S0-ADX-151

TALKING MAN

Also by Terry Bisson

WYRLDMAKER

TERRY BISSON

TALKING MAN

ARBOR HOUSE/NEW YORK

Copyright © 1986 by Terry Bisson
All rights reserved, including the right of reproduction
in whole or in part in any form. Published in the
United States of America by Arbor House Publishing
Company and in Canada by Fitzhenry & Whiteside Ltd.

Designed by Richard Oriolo

Manufactured in the United States of America

10 9 8 7 6 5 4 3 2 1

Library of Congress Cataloging in Publication Data

Bisson, Terry.
Talking man.

I. Title.
PS3552.I7736T3   1986   813'.54   86-3489
ISBN: 0-87795-813-0

*For Peter Rabbit,
Teacher*

1

THERE ARE TWO WAYS to tell a wizard. One is by the blue light that plays around his tires when he is heading north on wet pavement under the northern lights, his headlights pointed toward the top of the world that so many talk about but so few have actually seen.

The other is by his singing.

Talking Man was a wizard who had a small junkyard on the side of a hill on the Kentucky Tennessee line. He sold parts and cars, swapped guns and cars, fixed farm machinery and cars, dug ginseng and mayapple in season, and had an 1,100-pound allotment of burley tobacco which he let his daughter raise. He kept no chickens, no hogs and no dogs.

Talking Man wore a gray felt hat that was black at

the front where he used the brim for a handle, and an old sport coat that had started out charcoal with salmon stitching but was now just gray, with darker gray around the pockets, which sagged with wrenches, spark plugs, vise-grips and sometimes a little gun. Talking Man walked bent over, as if he were always about to get into a car that might arrive at any moment.

Perhaps because it was hard, even impossible, to see his eyes under his hat, he was good at swapping things.

He was good at fixing things. Talking Man could persuade a redbelly Ford tractor to start on a bone-cold February morning just by shaking a two-by-four at it, as if it were a smart mule. He could take the knock out of a poured-bearing Chevrolet with a set of ⅜-inch sockets and a wood file in an afternoon; he could free a stuck valve by pouring pond water through a carburetor, set points with cigarette papers, and sharpen a chainsaw without a file by passing the bar through a green-persimmon fire and singing a certain unhearable, to most people, song. Once, in Russellville, he jump-started a Negro preacher's car from his pickup without cables by jamming the bumpers together for a ground and then connecting the positive poles of the two batteries with his hands. His wife, Laurel Ann, sat in the truck frowning, angry because magic made her scared, and being scared made her angry; meanwhile their six-year-old, Crystal, held her ears against the singing not even her mother could hear.

That was ten years ago, before Laurel Ann was killed in a car wreck and Talking Man didn't get a scratch.

Talking Man was considered a fair welder, which meant he got exactly the same amount of work as a good welder would get. He knew the three ways to weld a gas tank so it wouldn't blow up (fill it with gas, fill it with water, fill it with exhaust fumes).

He was old.

He looked anywhere between forty-five and sixty, but he was older than that. He was older than the hills. He was older than the words people used or the things they talked about with them, older than the ground he hunkered down on when he was making a trade, older than older than stone. Talking Man was so old that, watching the buzzards float overhead, he could remember not only before there were buzzards, but before there were birds, before there were plants between the stones on the shore. Since time, like the world, is round, he could remember forward as well as backward: He could remember after the birds were gone, even their memories gone, their white bones piled up in drifts like snow, the air too weak for flying anymore.

Talking Man was a wizard from the end of time.

There, where the world ends in one endless moment, in a seamless black tower called Elennor, on the gravel shore of a gravel sea, in the light of the rings that once were the moon, Talking Man dreams the dream that is the world. He is dreaming it today. Beside him stands the white-gowned Dgene: She is his lover, his sister, his other, for it is nothing if not lonely at the end of time, and he dreamed her to dream him, for each without the other is only a dreamer and not a dream.

On the ledge in front of them is the owl that separates things and dreams. Look at it and it is two. Pick it up and it is one. But do not turn it, do not turn it, for the world turns with it.

At one end of time is the tower, Elennor, and at the

other is the city Edminidine. Between them is everything that is ever dreamed; and around them, nothing. Nothing is as cold as the cold between the stars. Nothing is the stuff that dreams are dreamed to undo. Nothing is undreamed, until Dgene dreamed it; unfelt, until she felt it; unbeen, until she turned to it and held it to her heart; a substance slick like water and sticky like fire and as cold as the cold between the stars.

She called into being the unbeen, and once it is dreamed the stars themselves are in danger.

It would have thrilled her to the bottom of her soul if Talking Man had dreamed of dreaming her a soul.

To turn around at the end of time takes a thousand thousand years, and when she turned around Talking Man was gone.

To turn around at the end of time takes a thousand thousand years, and when she turned around the unbeen was gone.

To turn around at the end of time takes a thousand thousand years, and when she turned around the owl was gone.

Talking Man knew what had happened when he took her hand and her fingernails were gone; under the folds of her white, white gown, the tips of her breasts were smooth without nipples; her eyes were as deep and storyless as the sea.

Talking Man knew that what she had touched was the unbeen he had been dreamed to dream away. Since the beginning of things, which begin in the city Edminidine, he had guarded against this day. He had been warned, for he was not the first of his kind, only the last. He had even found a jar to hide it in. So he tore it from her and fled. He also took the owl, for without it Dgene couldn't follow him.

And it almost worked. Except that he fell in love with the world he dreamed, and he gave himself away. Perhaps he had dreamed too well . . .

Still, it took Dgene a million years to find him and another million to bring him back.

She found him living in a house trailer on the side of a hill with his daughter, Crystal, sixteen.

2

ON SATURDAY MORNING, CRYSTAL was disking the tobacco ground on the far side of the hill from the house trailer and the shop when she heard shots. It was the middle of May and May is hot on the Kentucky Tennessee line. In the bottoms below, Six Mile Creek had overflowed its banks and was shining silvery through the trees like a fallen section of sky. Meanwhile, the sky above was as blue as Crystal had always imagined the sea might be.

The first two shots were pops, like a .22, and she didn't pay much attention to them since Talking Man was always fooling around with guns. He was probably just knocking a can off a fence post, an important part of a swap. Besides, Crystal had her hands full with the tractor, an old hand-clutch John Deere "A" that made even a daydreamer's job like disking complicated.

Crystal was not a small girl, but her legs still weren't long enough to reach the brakes. At the end of each row, she had to jump down from the seat onto the gearbox, then stand up on the right brake to make the giant tractor turn; close the throttle down; pull back out of the way while the steering wheel spun and the front end skated across the ground; then jump off the brake before the tractor ran over its own disk; crack the throttle wide open again; and jump back up into the heaving, jolting, hard green metal seat. There is no meaner, stronger, heavier machine than the "A." All green and all cast iron, it is like a cross between a grasshopper and a locomotive, and Crystal loved its big two-cylinder boom chunk boom chunk boom chunk boom. Like any normal person, she hated farming, but she loved the spring smells of gasoline and plowed ground.

Of course, she wasn't a farmer. Tobacco was all she grew.

The next shot was a crack as loud as thunder. There were two more pops, then another thundering crack.

Crystal looked up, then down. She bit her lip. She pulled back on the lever to disengage the clutch, and the big John Deere heaved to a stop in the soft dirt in the middle of the field. She closed the throttle, pushing the lever on the steering column forward, so that the engine slowed to a quieter boom chunk chunk chunk boom chunk chunk.

There was another loud shot. Then a long silence. Then another shot.

Reaching behind her, Crystal found the grass rope

that was tied to the back of the seat and yanked on it, pulling the pin that connected the disk to the tractor. She jammed the gearbox into fifth, the "A's" high road gear. She pulled back on the throttle and jammed the clutch forward and the John Deere reared like a horse, then set its front end down and started gaining speed diagonally across the plowed field, the two giant bucket-size cylinders booming, the arm-long crank-throws pulling, faster and faster: boom chunk boom boom chunk boom boom boom chunk boom boom boom.

Crystal left the plowed ground and followed the fencerow around the hill. She stood on the gearbox and held onto the wheel for dear life. She knew she was going too fast for the high, narrow machine known throughout the Upper Mid South as the Widowmaker, but she was scared. Something told her this wasn't just Talking Man fooling around with guns. The big noise had sounded like a .357 or a shotgun.

The fencerow met the dirt road that angled up the hill, and Crystal slowed to cross the shallow ditch—first dropping her narrow front wheels into the ditch, then nosing them up the other side onto the road. As her back wheels settled into the ditch, first one and then the other, she heard a rushing sound from up the hill, like wind. She looked up but she couldn't see the trailer, hidden behind the trees.

Just then a car hurtled down the road out of the trees straight for the tractor, which was broadside across the road. Crystal could hear the wild howl of a carburetor sucking air. She stood up on the left brake and cracked the throttle open. The John Deere reared back and swung its long nose into the air and out of the way, like a buck sniffing the wind, just as the car sped past, missing it by inches. In the dust, Crystal couldn't see how close it had been, but she felt the wind on her bare ankles and on the back of her neck.

It was a white car, a hardtop, she couldn't tell what kind—driven by a woman wearing a white scarf over snow-white hair and holding a gun in one hand.

Crystal heard a whooosh like birds taking off and another boom like thunder, and then the car disappeared down the hill. She sat down in the green metal seat. She felt scared, then angry, then amazed. She'd just been shot at for the first time in her life.

The John Deere accelerated slowly but steadily up the hill in fifth, and by the time Crystal got to the flat part of the road near the trailer it was running wide open, about 20 miles per hour. The screen door was open, but Crystal drove past and pulled up in front of Talking Man's shop, twenty yards on the other side of the trailer.

The tractor was a flywheel cranker that only Talking Man could start, so Crystal left it idling and ran inside.

She stopped in the darkness just inside the open door. The shop was a pole shed large enough for three cars, with a dirt floor and barky walls of cull lumber. The only light came from the door and from a trouble light underneath a pickup that was jacked up. The only sound came from Talking Man's '48 Chevy radio nailed to the wall in the back. Dickie Lee was singing "Nine Million, Nine Hundred Ninety-Nine Thousand, Nine Hundred Ninety-Nine Tears to Go." There was the smell of gunpowder and electricity in the air.

The pickup was Cleve Townsend's '61 GMC, which was unusual for a truck that old because it had an automatic transmission, put in after he lost his left foot in a hay baler, and no left door: Townsend had had Talking Man take it off last summer, since he only used the truck around the farm, and it made it easier getting in and out. Talking Man had been replacing a leaking transmission line. The Weldwood panel he used as a creeper was under the truck, dusted white with what looked like flour. The trouble light lay on it in a pool of what looked like blood.

Crystal got down on her hands and knees and crawled under the truck. The red was transmission oil. The white was snow. She tried to switch the light off but it wasn't even on. The glow was coming from somewhere in the air, and even as she watched, it faded away. She scooped up a little snow with the side of her finger and backed away toward the door.

Talking Man was nowhere to be seen.

There is nothing that idles slower than a John Deere "A." It was shaking in the May sunshine. Boom chunk chunk boom chunk chunk chunk. Crystal leaned against it. Now she felt really scared. The snow was still there on her finger. Snow in May in Kentucky. She shook it off. She knew what it was, and she knew it meant something was wrong, even though she hadn't seen any of it since her mother had died.

Magic.

She went into the house trailer and looked in every room, even though she didn't expect to find Talking Man there. There was nothing in his room but the double bed he'd shared with her mother until three years ago. He didn't have many clothes, and he didn't read any magazines. Crystal's room was nicer, with a shelf of books and a shelf of records. In the front room the TV was on with no sound. On top of it were the little horses her mother had collected from as far away as Washington, D.C., all facing the same way as the screen. But something was missing. The owl. It was just a little china owl, but Crystal always noticed it, because the only time she'd ever gotten a spanking from Talking Man was once when she'd touched it.

Now it was gone. Outside, the tractor shook in the sun. Through the open door, Crystal could see trucks passing on the moon-colored interstate at the bottom of the hill.

Talking Man had only used magic when he thought no one was around who was big enough to notice. This was foolish, since little girls especially remember cars floating through the air or woodstoves that stay hot with no fire in them, like the one in Talking Man's shop that he was too lazy to get wood for.

But the thing Crystal remembered most about the magic was the fights. Magic had made her mother furious. She always said it would get him in trouble. Her name was Laurel, and she'd called herself Mountain Laurel, hoping to become a star in Nashville, before she met Talking Man. She had worn bright dresses, and Talking Man's gray had set them off, the way the woods make the redbuds seem brighter.

Then there was the car wreck.

Talking Man came to Crystal's school the day her mother died. They sat in the U-shaped driveway at the school, and Talking Man had been the one who'd cried. The tears ran down the cracks on his face but he didn't make a sound. They were in his '56 Oldsmobile with the chrome-striped dash, and ever since, dashboards had seemed deliberately sad to Crystal, made to look sad like graveyards.

There had been no more fights and no more magic after that—until yesterday.

Talking Man had used magic to fix the windshield on a Mustang late Friday afternoon. Crystal had been surprised but hadn't said anything. The boy that owned the Mustang had been skeptical, and she had laughed trying to imagine his face when he saw it worked. Could her mother have been right? Could that have led to this? The shots. The strange woman. Talking Man gone . . .

Crystal felt like crying. The neighbors would help, but what would she tell them? She didn't have any friends to call. On the schoolbus she sat alone. She didn't have a boyfriend. Her only relatives were her mother's family, and she didn't even know where they lived, somewhere in Tennessee.

She turned off the TV. Talking Man always left it on. Even though he never watched it, he let it flicker like a fire. Crystal always turned it off. As a child, she'd thought the little people would get all used up.

Then she heard a car coming up the hill.

It was the Mustang.

3

WILLIAM TILDEN HENDRICKS WILLIAMS'S cousin hated to loan him his Mustang, but blood is thicker than water. On Friday morning in Bowling Green, he got the monthly call from his mother. He wrote the message for Williams on the front of a ten of hearts from a discarded deck in his neat, McLean County hand and gave it and the Mustang keys to a watcher (not a player) who owed him a favor. He told him to take them both to Judy's Blue Grass Castle on the bypass and give them to a guy in an O (for Owensboro) jacket who would be at the Missile Command machine at the front of the restaurant, inserting an inheritance that was supposed to take him through college and law school into a slot that would only take it a quarter at a time.

Williams was there but he wasn't at the machine. They had taken it out that morning, and he was through with Missile Command anyway. He was sitting at the counter reading the car ads in the *Warren County/Bowling Green Buy Lines*. He hadn't been to class in five weeks or on campus in three, so the issue of school was settled, and he was glad. He had never wanted to be a lawyer. What he wanted to do was get a car and a girl and settle down. He had worked two summers as an R&R (remove and replace) man at Walt's transmission shop, and Walt had told him he had a job when he wanted it.

Williams was from what his grandfather arrogantly (but accurately) described as the bourbon branch of a white whiskey family: the eldest son of an eldest son. His father, Junior Williams, was a lawyer who practiced real estate and county politics; a Kentucky Colonel along with twenty-five other Democrats every year who didn't want a county job and didn't need a load of gravel. Junior's father had actually practiced what they'd called, at the time, law. His father, Williams's great-grandfather, had been named Tilden Hendricks after the 1876 Democratic ticket that had, even in defeat, withdrawn the federal troops from the South and defeated Reconstruction; he had spent his second twenty years rewriting land titles, for law in Kentucky is about nothing if not about land. His father had also been a colonel, of the original but no more genuine sort, commissioned by the secessionist Confederate State Congress in Bowling Green along with twenty-five other western Kentucky planters' sons with six or more slaves, two or more horses, a cap and ball pistol, and enough sense to load and fire it.

His mother had been a Todd. Riverboat people.

They called defeating Reconstruction "saving the land," but the land had been the first thing to go. The slaves didn't get it but the banks did. First the pasture on the knobs near Jewel City, where the Pond and Green rivers come together. Then the timber. Then the great Green River bottoms themselves, where hemp was uncertain, cotton a disaster, but tobacco and corn dependable no matter how late the ground dried out. A small distillery, started by Williams's great-great-uncle Roy in 1909, had gone in 1922, and the sawmill right after the war. The new Roosevelt bridge put the ferry, which came with the middle Todd daughter, out of business. All Williams remembered was the tobacco business and the smell of the giant barns where he had helped his grandfather strip burley before Thanksgiving and one-sucker after; he had never smoked, because tobacco never tasted as good as it smelled in the barns. His other grandfather's packet boat, the Gayoso, had gone in 1951 with the last of the river traffic. Especially built for the long shallows and narrow chutes of the Green and Barren rivers, it had carried wrought iron over the windows to knock away the branches on the turns, where the channel went under the out-leaning giraffe-barked sycamores.

The Williams place itself had gone in '72. Soybeans got so profitable that the barns were all torn down and even the old backyard was plowed and planted. But Williams didn't see any of this happen. Like millions of others, his folks had long since moved to town. He grew up in Owensboro in a house built the year he was born, on a street built the year he was born; even the two skinny maple trees in the front yard were exactly his age.

Now all that was left after a hundred and fifty years

of timber and slavery, tobacco and slavery, whiskey and slavery, trading and buying and selling and lawing, was a trust fund that was supposed to see that the eldest son of every eldest son got a law degree from the University of Kentucky in Lexington. But things had changed since Junior went to school, and now eighteen hundred dollars was barely enough for a BA from Western Kentucky State College in Bowling Green, much less a law degree from the university in Lexington.

So Williams found himself on the bypass in Bowling Green, having made it through one year, from Charlemagne to Napoleon, before discovering Missile Command. He was what is known in the Upper Mid South as a dreamer, more interested in defending the cities on the dark Nintendo plain than in his studies. His eighteen hundred dollars was down to fifty now. Mastering the game had taken most of his third semester.

"Your mother's awake," the note said. The Mustang keys explained themselves.

Williams's mother slept for weeks at a time, waking for only a few hours every month. It was a hereditary condition that sometimes skipped a generation, but never affected more than one Todd at a time. Her sisters, who visited her every other day in her blue-papered upstairs bedroom, were skilled at telling when she was going to wake up and always wrote Williams to let him know; or, if he had no address, called his cousin, who also lived in Bowling Green and had a car.

It was a robin-egg blue '66 Mustang with a Cleveland 351 that Williams's cousin hardly drove and never raced. He paid a guy to mount the tires by hand so the tire machine wouldn't scratch the Centerline wheels. He wouldn't run it through a car wash because of the brushes. He only loaned it to Williams to visit his mother when she was awake because his own mother, Williams's mother's sister, had made that a condition of buying it for him.

Williams drove to Owensboro and spent most of the day with his mother. Instead of telling her he was dropping out of school, he decided to put it off. It was late afternoon when he kissed her goodbye. She was lying in bed in a blue robe. Outside, the dogwood was in its last mad flush. Downstairs, the Mustang gleamed in the drive like one of those dogs that know they are worth more than their owner. The TV flickered like a window on another, even smaller, world.

"You're studying hard?" she said.

"Promise," Williams lied.

He drove back toward Bowling Green on the Green River Parkway, the same way he had driven up, because his cousin didn't want the Mustang subjected to any stray gravel or branches, such as might be lurking along the edges of an ordinary highway. Driving on the parkway was part of the deal. The road was deserted, as always, and driving the high-cammed Mustang on it was like flying: swooping through the cuts and slashes in the hills and over the bottomlands like a mark on a map, with no need to worry about the terrain.

Near Morgantown, the parkway crosses the Green River on a new, high, white concrete bridge that spans all the way from the Ohio County bluffs, across the dark water of what is rumored to be the deepest river in the world, across the half-mile crescent-shaped bottomlands barely colored with new corn, to Butler County to the south. Below the new bridge, Williams saw the old iron highway bridge, still in use, and beneath it were the cable towers for the old ferry landing. On an artificial rise by the south-bank ferry landing, which before had been a packet landing and wood station, stood the house where his father had been born and his grandfather had died. It was empty now. The yard was planted in beans. The hollow fluted columns ordered from Atlanta had fallen off, and the brick facing was peeling away, uncovering the reality behind the mansion—a two story dogtrot cabin of silvery yellow poplar logs.

Williams had driven over the old house on the parkway a thousand times, but he hadn't been there since he was a kid. There were no boats on the river, no cars or houses in either direction: only dark hills and dark woods, for just as the bottomlands had been taken by the soybean businessmen, the little hillside farms had been reclaimed by the possums, the strip mines, the little cedars and the bean-fed, lookful deer.

Looking down, Williams decided his cousin would never know the difference if he got off at the Morgantown exit, looped back two miles and finished the trip to Bowling Green on 431, so he could drive past the old place. Looking back later, he could see that this was where he began his trip to the North Pole.

4

IT WAS A BEAUTIFUL Friday afternoon in early May, and Williams was glad to be off the four-lane. The world which had looked so empty from up there was actually filled with porches and clotheslines, kids and new gardens.

He rolled down the windows and Conway Twitty came on the radio. Then a Peabody coal truck passed, and a lump of coal hit the windshield like a shot.

It broke right in the center.

The tiny hole was the size of a BB, but the spiderweb of cracks was bigger than a man's hand.

Williams pulled over to think. He could lie, but his cousin would never believe him. There were no coal trucks on the parkway. He could try and get it replaced. At least it was the glass and not the paint.

Williams tried two junkyards, one in Morgantown and one in Bowling Green, before he found a junkman willing to take an interest in his problem and explain that there was only one chance of finding a '66 Mustang windshield this side of Nashville and $200, and that was a little country garage right off the interstate on the Kentucky Tennessee line run by an old-timer named Talking Man. He wouldn't have it but he might know where to get it. The best way to get there was to cut off the interstate illegally through a hole in the fence just past the WELCOME TO KENTUCKY sign.

Williams found the hole in the fence as the sun was touching the tops of the hills. The afternoon was ending and it was getting ready to start getting dark.

The junkyard, up a narrow dirt road, was a disappointment. There was a house trailer and a pole shed on a hillside, at the edge of a steep field filled with ragweed, trash cedar and old cars.

Williams pulled up in front of the shed. There was a flickering light inside. A radio was playing and a man was welding a plow beam without a mask, his hat pulled down over his eyes. A teenage girl came out of the house trailer, and Williams explained to her what he wanted and said he was looking for a certain Talking Man. She went into the shed and pulled the welder's sleeve, and he cut off the torch and walked out into the sun.

The girl stood to one side while Williams explained all over again what he wanted. Talking Man nodded, found a cigarette loose in one pocket, straightened it, lit it, but never said anything. He was a hillbilly with a slouch hat pulled down over his face, wearing a greasy sport coat and brown boots with no laces.

He put his hand on the girl's shoulder and cocked his head to one side.

"He says there's a '64 up by the fence," the girl said, "but he says he thinks hit's busted." Williams could see that this was one of those deals where a tall man was called Shorty or a fat man, Slim.

The girl was kind of pretty, though.

"Ask him if he minds if I go look," Williams said. "If there's a chance it's good, I might take it off his hands."

"He says hit's all right." When she spoke she used the old-fashioned *hit* for *it*. "He says would you give a hundred dollars?"

Williams said, "Let me look at it." That was way too high, and he only had fifty dollars anyway; but if it was good, he could always talk the old guy down.

Talking Man shrugged and went back into the shed, and the light started flickering again. Williams started walking up the field between the cars, and to his surprise the girl walked with him, being careful not to get her shoes muddy. They were K-Mart imitation Adidas. The junkyard was hardly worth the name; it was just ragged rows of cars, all facing north, that had been in the field so long that sassafras trees were growing through the trunks and hoods. The Mustang at the fence at the top of the field was a '64, all right; the windshield looked good from a distance, but when they got close Williams saw it was cracked in almost the same place as his cousin's.

"Hit has to be a '66?" the girl asked.

"'Sixty-five to '67, according to the book," said Williams.

"There's a big junkyard down on Dixie Highway."

"That's the guy who sent me here."

"Oh."

Williams decided to give up, much as he hated to. His cousin probably wouldn't kill him, even though once when they were kids he had pulled a gun on him for wrecking his bicycle. It was almost dark, and even if he found a windshield, it was too late to put it in. Luckily, since it was Friday, his cousin would be playing cards all night, and he didn't have to return the car and face the music until morning. He decided there was no sense worrying about it until then.

Walking back, down a row of tractor parts and tobacco setters, the girl said, "Sorry." It seemed so important to him.

Williams said, "Thanks," and asked her her name.

She said it was Crystal, after the country singer and sister of Loretta Lynn, who her mother had met once.

He said, Loretta?

She said, Crystal. She said she was a singer, too.

He said, Crystal?

She said, her mother, Laurel Ann; musical stage name, Mountain Laurel.

Williams had never heard of her, but of course he didn't say so. He could tell from the way she said it she was dead. Williams told Crystal he worked in a transmission shop in Owensboro. He didn't like to tell girls he went to college.

Then Williams saw the most beautiful car he had ever seen.

It was parked behind Talking Man's shop. It was a red and white '62 Chrysler New Yorker two-door hardtop with a red and white leatherette interior. The tires were up but old and dry-rotted. It looked like the car hadn't been run for a long time. The seats and the dash were covered with fine dust, but even through the dust the dashboard was gorgeous: clear plastic dials standing upright on a black field, covered with a clear dome like a city in science fiction.

Williams walked around the car twice before he touched it. He opened the hood and saw that the rocker covers and carburetor were off. A grass sack was stuffed in the manifold. There was no battery.

It was the car he wanted to buy.

"Hit's not for sale," Crystal said.

"Who said I wanted to buy it?"

"I can just tell. There's only a few things he won't sell."

Williams shrugged. What could he do with fifty dollars anyway? It would take two hundred just to get it running. They walked around to the front of the shed. Talking Man was hunkered down in the doorway, humming to himself, mixing something in a coffee can with a large screwdriver. He stirred it and it smoked a little. While Williams and Crystal watched, he threw in some dirt and a pinch of Solder Seal, then poured in a little brake fluid.

"What's he doing?" Williams asked.

Crystal looked puzzled herself.

Talking Man looked up at her and then back down. He stirred the can, still humming, and it smoked some more.

"I think he's fixing to fix your windshield," Crystal said. Talking Man quit stirring and walked over to the Mustang and smeared the black mixture onto the windshield over the cracks, using the screwdriver like a spatula. It steamed a little as it went on.

"What in the hell's he doing?"

"He says if hit doesn't work, you can get your money back, but he says hit's worth a try."

"What money?"

"The hundred dollars."

On the way to Bowling Green, leaning out the window so that he could see to drive, Williams could hardly believe he had paid forty dollars for the glob of mud on the windshield. He laughed to himself; another way of looking at it was that he had talked the old man down from a hundred dollars. That made it less-than-half-price mud.

It was a funny story but not one he had anybody to tell to.

He picked up a six-pack and fell asleep in front of the TV. He slept in a chair all night, dreaming of the white Chrysler and, oddly enough, the girl. He got up early the next morning to take the car to his cousin's and face the music. But when he scraped the mud off the glass with his fingertips, he couldn't find the break. The windshield was fixed.

5

THE JOHN DEERE SHOOK in the sun like an old dog scratching. Boom chunk chunk boom chunk chunk boom chunk chunk boom. It was Saturday morning. Williams couldn't hear anything the girl was saying. He reached up to shut off the tractor, but she shook her head and led him over near the shop door, where it was quieter.

"Hit looks okay," she said, looking at the Mustang's windshield. "What's the problem."

"It's fixed," he said. "I didn't come to get my money back. I just came to see . . . How'd he do that?" Williams peered into the dark shop. There was a funny smell. "Where's he at?"

Crystal couldn't decide what not to tell him, so she told him almost everything. She said she'd been disking her tobacco patch. She told him about the shots and the car that had almost run her down, but she left out the snow.

"Now Talking Man is gone. Don't shut off the tractor, because if you do I can't get hit started again. He's the only one in the whole county that can start hit," she said. She was wearing a Burley Belt hat and older, dirtier fake Adidas than yesterday.

Williams walked into the shed to look around. It was dark and the radio was playing Conway Twitty. The air smelled like electricity and gunpowder. Williams knelt down beside the GMC pickup and Crystal knelt beside him.

"Isn't there a light?" he said.

She pulled on the cord and dragged out the trouble light and switched it on. The glow she had seen earlier under the truck was gone. They crawled under the truck. Now she told him about the snow. It was gone, but the air was still cold. Transmission oil was dripping onto the Weldwood sheet, and Williams saw why: a line was disconnected. He rolled over on his back and hooked it up and the dripping stopped.

Crystal had gone back outside. He found her leaning against the John Deere which was still booming and shaking faithfully in the sun. He saw that she was about to cry, and without thinking he reached up and shut it off.

She burst into tears.

Williams backed away.

"I told you not to shut hit off," she said. "I'll never get that tractor going again. I'll never get my tobacco set."

He tried to apologize, but she suddenly held up her hand. "Shhh!"

"What?"

She heard singing. It was far away and fading, but she remembered it even though she hadn't heard it since she was a little girl. It was Talking Man. It was that scary magic sound he made. It sounded like it was up behind the trailer. Then it was gone.

Williams didn't hear anything.

Crystal headed toward the trailer, across the bare dirt littered with parts, tires, hubcaps and wood scraps. Williams followed her. There was everything but grass in Talking Man's yard.

The porch was three concrete blocks on top of six concrete blocks. Inside, there was a kitchen/dinette/living room with a built-in couch and a window overlooking the yard and the dirt road and the interstate in the distance. Trucks rolled north endlessly. The sink was piled with dishes. The couch was stained with grease in one spot in front of the TV; it looked like Talking Man's ghost.

The nineteen-inch TV set was playing with no sound.

"Was this on?" Williams asked, looking for clues.

"I turned hit off," Crystal said. "Hit comes back on."

There were two other rooms. Talking Man's was just a bed with an old blanket under a narrow, high window. Crystal's was larger and neater. There was a picture on the wall of a woman wearing a fringed skirt, standing in front of another picture of mountains, holding a Gibson Hummingbird guitar.

Crystal sat down on the couch next to the Talking Man dark spot. She found a cigarette in a crumpled pack of Camels on the coffee table and lit one. On top of the TV, a collection of little glass horses had been knocked over, and Williams set them up.

"There's supposed to be a little owl," Crystal said. "Hit's gone."

Williams noticed a funny sound.

"Hear that?" Crystal sat up straight.

This time Williams could hear it. Through the open window in the rear of the trailer, from the back of the hill, from beyond the junkyard and down in the woods: a wild high mournful magic singing, unlike anything he had ever heard before.

The singing didn't get louder or softer as they approached the top of the hill behind the trailer. Once Williams had heard it, it wouldn't go away; it seemed to come from inside him rather than outside, from between his bones. Crystal seemed glad that he had heard it, too. She ran ahead in the junkyard, then waited for him to catch up. He noticed she ran like a girl, and walked like a woman.

The junkyard ended at a fence at the top of the hill. They slipped between two strands of barbed wire into the woods. The woods were clean, like woods where cattle have been; then the brush got thicker as they crossed the top of the hill and started down the other side. It got steeper. Williams held onto a cloud-white hornbeam, the strongest tree for its size in the world, and looked down. The bluff was almost as steep as a cliff but still covered with ferns and brush and trees. At the bottom there was a flash of water. They slid down from tree to tree, staying on their feet, first Crystal going ahead and then Williams, until they reached the last ledge just above the creek. Crystal held up her hand and stopped Williams.

The singing came from right under her feet.

He tiptoed down to stand beside her. He grabbed a

tree and leaned over and looked down. They were standing over a cave the size of a door laid on its side. The singing was no louder, but it was definitely coming from inside the cave.

They climbed down and stood in front of the cave entrance on a rock in the shallow stream. Cool air came out and it looked like a mouth singing. Williams didn't like it. Crystal bent down and looked in.

"There's his feet," she said.

"So tell him to come on."

"I expect we have to go in and get him."

It was lighter inside the cave than Williams had expected. Talking Man was leaning against the damp limestone wall just inside the entrance. His feet were splayed out so he wouldn't fall, and his hands were jammed into the pockets of his coat. Deep under his hat, his eyes were closed. His mouth was open slightly; the singing was a sort of low humming, no louder here than when they'd heard it at the top of the hill.

"Take his feet," Crystal said. She took his shoulders and they carried him out into the sunlight. A gun, some bills and a little owl fell out of Talking Man's jacket into the shallow water. She scooped them up quickly. Williams recognized the two folded twenties he'd given Talking Man last night. They leaned him against the creekbank and switched ends, Williams taking the bony old shoulders, and started up the hill. It wasn't as bad as Williams had expected. The old man was stiff and light, like a branch, and they carried him easily between them, going up from tree to rock to tree, stopping to rest twice. Talking Man's arms hung at his side, but not loosely enough to drag on the ground, and his head stayed stiffly upright. Williams would have thought he was dead except for the singing.

"Does he get like this very much?"

"No," Crystal said. "And I know what you're think-ing."

"I'm not thinking anything."

They were at the fence. They leaned Talking Man against a fence post—it didn't seem right to lay him down—and Williams climbed through; then together they passed him over the top. For a moment, while Crystal climbed through the fence, Williams held the old man by himself in his arms, surprised at how little he weighed.

They carried him down between the junk cars and into the trailer. They set him in front of the TV, which was back on. He sat stiffly, leaning back hard against the cushion with his hands jammed in his pockets. Williams couldn't see under his hat to tell if his eyes were still closed. He followed Crystal out to the front stoop, where she was sitting down fishing a cigarette out of a crumpled pack. The owl and the gun were on her lap. The gun was a little Iver Johnson .32.

He sat down beside her.

"I know what you're thinking," she said, "and you can just stop thinking hit."

"What?"

"You're thinking he's got a dope patch or a still down in the woods."

"No, honest, I'm not," Williams said. "Honest. I just think it's weird. It's like the windshield. He was sort of singing when he mixed up that mud."

"He's not drunk," Crystal said.

"So he's not drunk." Williams shrugged. "You better clean that gun up or it'll rust," he said, trying to change the subject.

"He's always singing whenever he's doing something.

The singing means he's doing something. I just don't always know what."

Williams looked behind him into the trailer. It didn't look to him like Talking Man was doing anything, but he wasn't about to say it.

"Why don't you let me clean that gun up," he said. He reached for the gun, and Crystal jumped up, thinking he was reaching for the owl, which Talking Man had never let anybody, not even her mother, touch.

"This goes on the TV," she said. She put it there. "And I can clean a gun, for your information." She wiped it off, but that was all, and slipped it into Talking Man's pocket. Williams noticed she kept the two twenties. It was almost lunchtime. "There's one thing I wish you would help me do, though. If that transmission in Cleve Townsend's pickup was hooked up, I could go pull my tobacco plants and be ready to set my tobacco as soon as Talking Man wakes up. I'll fix us some lunch."

TO GROW TOBACCO, FIRST you make a plant bed. Find a patch of new ground along the edge of the woods, ten feet wide by a hundred feet long; break it up, and let it lay all winter; in late February, hit it again and then rake it fine. In March, stack brush on it and burn it to kill the weed seeds, or, if you are modern, gas it—cover it with plastic sealed down with dirt around the edges, and pop open three cans to fill the plastic with white poison fog. In late March, take off the plastic or rake away the ashes, and work up the ground finer and smoother than any garden or golf course could ever be. Tobacco seeds are smaller than poppy seeds and cost five dollars for half a quarter of a teaspoonful, making them one of the most expensive substances on the planet. Mix them with fertilizer, or fireplace ashes if you are old fashioned, so they will spread evenly across the plant bed. Then cover the bed with a thin white cotton cloth like a bandage that will warm and protect the tiny plants. By the end of March the south sides of Kentucky's hillsides look like they have been in a fight, each with its own Band-Aid. After a month, the cloth is rolled away. If the gas or the burning failed, you have a regular museum of weeds. If the gas worked but the seed failed, you have a nice clean strip of reddish dirt. If for some unexplained reason everything went right, you have a carpet of tiny yellow-green plants, each with two leaves the size of dimes. Let them grow another month, until they are a half a foot high, then get the kids and the old folks to pull them, preferably in the morning when the ground is soft, but the afternoon's all right if the ground's not too dry. There will be plants enough to set your field, plus enough left over for the neighbors whose plants didn't come up, for the only insurance in such an uncertain business as tobacco is neighbors.

Talking Man never actually grew tobacco plants, he just pretended to. In late February, he would stretch a piece of tobacco cloth on the hillside up against the woods, where it was easy to see from the road, and leave it there until the middle of April. Then he would roll it up and put it away for next year. In late May, he would go around to the neighbors and pull enough plants to set his quarter of an acre. Nobody believed that Talking Man had actually tried and failed, but the spreading of the cloth showed his respect for appearances. Folks were glad to help him out, because they needed his help when the sun rode low in the sky and the tractors wouldn't start.

Crystal didn't like this system, but she had inherited

it when she began to grow the tobacco on her own. People respected the fact that she didn't like it, and liked the fact that she didn't try to change it.

Williams had to replace a section of hose and shorten a line to hook up the transmission. He secured the linkage rod with a finishing nail. The '48 Chevy radio on the wall apparently played all the time, since there was no way to change the station or turn it off. Meanwhile, Crystal was checking on Talking Man one more time. He was sitting in front of the TV, still singing. The TV was on again. She made two bologna sandwiches and turned it off again, just to see what would happen.

She threw two cardboard boxes into the back of the truck while Williams was still underneath, then waited in the driver's seat while he let it down. Then she backed it out of the shed. She handed him a sandwich and they ate sitting in the truck, sharing a Coke. It was too weird in the trailer.

"I might as well go along and help," Williams said. Pulling plants was one job in tobacco he didn't mind. He waited for her to scoot over, but she seemed to want to drive herself. She drove down the hill and out the same way he had come in, through the break in the fence and onto the interstate. He would have thought there would have been an easier way.

There was no door, and Williams could see the pavement racing by on the other side of her lap, harsh and moon-white. Williams wondered what would happen if the cops saw them. Of course, what would happen if they saw them cutting through the fence?

Crystal headed north and got off at the first exit. It was definitely spring and almost summer; the trees were new green and the plowed fields were red-brown. They drove to three farms before Crystal found what she was looking for. Beggars can't be choosers, but it pays to be particular about tobacco plants. If they are too big or too small, they will die before they take root, and Crystal had learned the hard way not to mix varieties that sucker and flower and ripen at different times.

Pulling plants is the easiest of all tobacco work, because you get to sit down; it and stripping are where the stories get told. Williams and Crystal sat in the sun at the edge of Leroy Willoughby's woods with the first box between them and filled it with plants standing upright shoulder to shoulder like singers in a church. Williams told her he'd helped his grandfather pull plants when he'd been so little his only job was to carry them to the boxes, one every minute or so. She told him she'd raised tobacco for three years and almost had enough money to go to business college in Bowling Green or Owensboro. Tobacco was a way to leave home, even though she wasn't sure she wanted to.

Starting on the second box, he told her the story of *Papillon,* from the scene where they cut a man open to get the jewels he has swallowed, to the end, where Papillon escapes for the last time into the sea. She had seen this movie too, and she liked hearing the story. She told him the story of *Heart Like a Wheel,* about drag-racing star Shirley Muldowney.

Williams told her he had gone out with the daughter of Cowboy Clark, the Indiana Kentucky dirt track driver, and Cowboy had let him drive ten laps in a claim race once. He was proud of this, but Crystal didn't seem impressed. She told him Talking Man used to drive dirt tracks in Owensboro and Madisonville, but she was too small to like watching. "I liked watching the boys pour Cokes better," she said. She was five. She sat where Talking Man had put her on the concessions counter. The boys gave her her own paper hat and let her put the straws in the drinks, the warm, mighty roaring of the engines behind her.

Williams asked her how Talking Man could fix a windshield with mud and she told him that was nothing. She had seen him float an engine through the air. "I was about six, you know when grown-ups think you aren't big enough to know anything, but really you are? I was sitting on the toolbench by the radio, and he was working on this old Chevy stock car with the hood off and a new engine outside in the back of the pickup. He stood back, and the engine floated in through the door, bobbing up and down like a barrel in the water."

"A whole engine?"

"Almost. The manifold and the carburetor were off, but everything else was there. Both heads were on. He guided hit down on the mounts with his hands. Just then he remembered me sitting there watching and he looked at me and grinned." She grinned. "Just then my mother came in, and they had a big fight and she took me in the trailer. Did your parents fight much?"

"All the time," Williams lied. His parents were hardly ever even in the same room. "So did the engine work?"

"I guess. I think hit was for racing. He won a few races before Mother made him quit. She could make him do anything."

The box was full of plants and Crystal stood up, brushing off her knees, then her seat. "She looked like an angel."

* * *

They stopped at the store on the way back, to buy fertilizer for setting. "Well, there's a problem, honey," said the blond fat woman who sat behind the potato chips eating potato chips.

"What's that?"

"Your daddy has to come in and sign for hit."

"I thought he had already done that."

"He might have forgot this year. He owes fifty dollars from last summer."

Crystal took the two twenties from her back pocket and handed them to the woman. "He said to give you this."

The woman slipped them into her back pocket. "It would still be better if he'd come in and sign. But you go on and take the fertilizer."

It was one of those stores that open up to a house in the back, and Williams could see a man at a kitchen table fooling with a CB radio. He looked up, and Williams saw that he was blind.

"All right, I guess," said Crystal. Williams picked up the five-gallon plastic can. Crystal charged a Snickers and they left, and split it in the truck.

They had to go north on the interstate, make a U-turn and head south again to find the hole in the fence.

"Well, you're fixed up now," Williams said, talking about the tobacco.

"I can't set anyway until he wakes up," Crystal said. "He has to start the tractor. Besides, hit takes three people."

"I have to go back to Bowling Green . . ."

"I didn't mean you," Crystal said. "One of the neighbors helps. I've already helped him set his."

"I have to take the car back. It's my cousin's. He'll be furious already. He was supposed to have it back this morning."

"I appreciate your helping already." Crystal looked out the back window at the two boxes in the truck bed. "They're pretty good-looking plants. I figure I've got two and a half days to get them in the ground."

"Maybe . . ." They were almost at the turn-off, and Williams decided to go ahead and say what he'd been thinking: "Maybe we should go to a movie sometime."

"How come?" She looked at him, surprised. "What's on?"

"I don't know," Williams said. She seemed dense sometimes. "I mean, after you get the tobacco set and I get a car. We could see what was on, you know . . ."

All of a sudden Crystal got it. A smile spread through her body, reaching up from the back of her knees to her face. "Like a date?"

"I don't know," he said, irritated. "Haven't you ever been on a date before?"

"Of course I have." She hadn't.

Williams could see the trailer and the junkyard on the side of the hill. While Crystal slowed down, he checked behind for cops, but the road was empty. Crystal was cutting across the median when a white hardtop came out of the cut in the fence, fast, crossed in front of them, and headed north.

"Who's that?" Williams asked.

A beautiful white-haired woman was driving, alone in the car. The strange thing was, Williams couldn't tell what kind of car it was. It looked a little like a Dodge from the front, but not quite; the grille wasn't frowning. From the side, it looked sort of like a Ford, with long, straight lines. From the back, it looked more like a Chevy, rounded and full.

"Who's that?" Williams asked again. Then he figured it out. "Was that her?"

"That was her."

Crystal looked worried. She maneuvered the truck through the hole in the fence, across the low ditch and onto the dirt road. Just then another car burst out of the trees ahead of them as sudden as a jumped deer, spun halfway around on the dirt, then straightened up and slipped through the hole and across the median. Leaving long black marks on the pavement and a familiar sharp bark in the air, it streaked north on the interstate while Crystal and Williams watched, her eyes wide with fear and his with astonishment.

It was the Mustang.

And driving it was Talking Man.

7

THE TRAILER DOOR WAS wide open. Inside, the TV was on. The little owl was gone from the top of the TV and all the little horses had been knocked onto the floor.

Williams followed Crystal back outside. The sun was setting. Crystal was standing beside the old John Deere, trying to light a cigarette, but her hands were shaking. Williams helped her and then looked around, surprised at how calm he felt. They couldn't follow him far in a pickup without a door. For a second he thought of calling the police, but then he thought better of it. They only made things worse. Besides, most of his cousin's friends were cops.

Then he noticed the Chrysler. It had been moved.

Instead of behind the shop, it was now sitting in front of the door.

"Where do you think he's going, Bowling Green?"

"Owensboro."

"How come?"

"That's just where he usually goes when he goes somewhere."

Williams left Crystal standing beside the John Deere and checked out the '62 Chrysler. The tires were up. The keys were in it. He got in and the seats felt cool, not like the car had been sitting in the sun all day. They had been dusted off. He turned the key but everything was dead. He got out and opened the hood. Talking Man had been working on the car, he could see; now there was a carburetor and both rocker covers were on, but there was no battery. He found a ½-inch and $\frac{9}{16}$-inch open end combination wrench and a vise-grip on the bench inside the garage door.

"What're you going to do?" Crystal asked.

"Take the battery out of the pickup," Williams said, angry now. "Put it in the Chrysler. Catch up with him. Get my car before he wrecks it or blows the engine all to pieces."

"Well, I'm going, too."

The battery was under the floorboard of the GMC. Crystal went into the trailer. By the time Williams had the battery in the Chrysler she was back outside, wearing a white pullover blouse and jeans with leather trim around the pockets and carrying a red-white-and-blue purse. She didn't come over to the car. She waited on the concrete block stoop with her purse on her knees.

Williams checked the oil and water. They were okay. He turned the key and the Chrysler started on the first lick. The oil pressure came right up. The engine sounded good. He pulled up in front of the trailer and reached across the seat to open the door for her.

"If anybody wrecks anything, hit won't be him," she said.

"Try the radio," Williams said. He didn't see any sense arguing about it.

They headed north. The Chrysler was smooth and quiet and powerful. The only thing that worried Williams was the dry-rotted tires. The thing he liked best was the dash. There was an oval console set behind and around the steering column—transparent on top, like a great plastic egg. Inside it, the dials sat upright like half moons imbedded in black, each glowing softly with phosphorescent light. They all worked: the oil pressure, the ammeter, the temperature, the gas. Even the lighter and the glove-compartment light worked. Everything but the radio, which was a disappointment. The light wouldn't even come on.

Crystal was quiet. She sat smoking, looking out at the people setting tobacco in the deepening twilight. It was the time of year when families worked late in the fields with spotlights on the tractors, the women and teenagers on the setters, the children sitting in the backs of the pickups, boys on one side, girls on the other, the fathers driving tractors in long straight rows, not out stealing boys' cars.

The road divides at Bowling Green, I-65 heading north and east to Louisville, and the Green River Parkway heading north and west to Owensboro, up the easy timbered slope of the Dripping Springs Escarpment. It got dark, and the little hillside farms gave way to the rough, underpopulated coal country of north Warren,

Butler, then Ohio counties. There were no other cars on the road, no lights in the hills.

They crossed the high bridge over the Green River at Morgantown, and far below, Williams saw the old two-story Williams place. He thought he saw a light in the window and he backed off the gas, surprised, but it was just a reflection.

"Look," said Crystal, pointing over the black hills. The moon had just come up, more than half full. Williams brought the Chrysler back up to speed—65, 75— and on into the darkness they sped.

There were the Pond River bottoms, and then more low clay hills.

"Do you know where to look in Owensboro?" Williams asked.

Crystal shook her head. They were coming down into the bottoms again. To the right, the old highway was almost as deserted as the parkway, with only a pickup or two. On both sides the Panther Creek swamps went on for miles, as black as if they'd been painted with night, but far from quiet. Crystal rolled her window down, and the air was wild with the screams of bugs and frogs.

Ahead, the red lights of the WOMI radio tower winked on and off, winked on and off. Crystal tried the radio again. No luck.

8

EVERY CITY HAS ITS dark and secret heart and Owensboro is no exception. The world thinks of it as a whiskey town, a tobacco town, a river town, an oil boomtown layered with subdivisions and shopping centers like skins and encircled in the cold concrete arms of new highways that go only from one side of town to the other. The earth knows it for its great yellow clay banks feeding the Ohio, which is always so hungry for dirt, or for its oldest inhabitant, the largest sassafras tree on the planet, older than anyone even suspects, which was a seedling child 20 thousand years ago when the river ran cold with melting ice and children's fathers still told stories about hunting buffalo with tusks who hunted men back. From nine to five, Owensboro is a tobacco market, the biggest west of Louisville, a maker of light bulbs and white-oak whiskey barrels, a loader of coal from the new bleak stretches to the south where the coal is not dug from the earth by men but ripped out by machines taller than cathedrals. Saturdays until noon, it's a car parts town. Sundays, it's a church-going town with the sweet smell of sour mash floating over the rooftops like a drinker's prayer. It's a border town perched on the high precipice edge of the South, where you can park downtown and see all the way across the muddy mile-wide Mason-Dixon line to the Indiana bottomlands, looming as wild and as northern in a boy's imagination as Alaska. It's a river-bottom town, where a rock the size of a hubcap is a boulder.

But in its dark and secret heart, Owensboro is a night town. It's a barbecue, half-pint, jukebox, parking lot, six-pack, glass-pack, steel guitar town that calls out to every hopeful heart in five counties every Saturday night, and gets answered. It's a stop and a half up the road from Nashville, and the bright lights leave a mark on its children—that hopeful look Crystal had seen in Williams's eye in the junkyard that reminded her of her mother.

It was Saturday night.

They sailed into Owensboro between two low hills. "Got any ideas?"

Crystal shook her head, so they cruised past the first cluster of drive-ins and bars, then down Triplett to Second Street, down near the river where the trees get bigger and the air gets darker. There is a routine to driving around Owensboro on Saturday night, and Williams knew it well: Out Second Street, through the old forgotten downtown, past the east end drive-ins and bars, then back on Fourth and south on Frederica, past the new shopping plazas and fast food restaurants. The Mustang was nowhere to be seen. Crystal sat by the door smoking and looking, saying not a word.

Williams stopped at a 7-Eleven in the south end for gas. While he pumped it Crystal went in to buy cigarettes. Out of the car, standing in line, in the bright lights through the big window, dressed up with her hair pulled back in a pony tail, he hardly recognized her. He went in to pay and bought a Snickers and walked back out with her. All cars look good on Saturday night, under the lights, and the red and white '62 Chrysler New Yorker hardtop was no exception.

Williams drove by his parents' house on Hill Street. He drove past the world's largest sassafras tree. Crystal sat leaning against the door while he made the circuit again. It only took a few minutes. He decided to widen the search. They drove to the Holiday Inn at the Y on the highway to Henderson, and back past the water tower, then turned down mysterious Crabtree and up wild, dark Ninth. They drove past the south side shopping centers, where the drive-ins were newer than the cars, and past the west end barbecues, where the parking lots were filled with pickups and Harleys.

Crystal tried the radio again while Williams drove in ever-widening circles to take in the places beyond the edges of town. He was beginning to get ready to give up when Crystal put her hand across his wrist and said, "There it is."

It wasn't the Mustang.

It was the white car, the weird one.

9

WILLIAMS WOULD HAVE DRIVEN past it if Crystal hadn't seen it. It was parked in the lot of a barbecue joint east of Owensboro on Highway 60. It was a white two-door hardtop. It had a square rear deck like a Ford and a wide grille like a Pontiac. It had flush door handles, modest fins, and a "dog corner" windshield in the style of the fifties. It looked a little like every car, but not exactly like any kind of car.

Williams walked around it once, then twice. It had Kentucky plates. There wasn't anything about it that was strange, yet there was nothing familiar. If it had been a custom job, at least one part would have been borrowed from another car. If it had been a Canadian version (he had read about these in a magazine) the sheet metal would have been familiar. It was weird. He hadn't touched it, so he put out his hand to the fender. It felt like any other car.

He looked inside. The interior was maroon and gray, plastic and plush, ornate and overdone like an Oldsmobile. Williams was shocked to see that cigarettes had been put out on top of the dash.

"Let's look inside." Crystal's voice surprised him. He thought she meant the car but she meant the restaurant. She was standing by the stairs, holding her purse in front of her with both hands. She looked different and Williams noticed she had put on lipstick.

The stairs to the Night Owl led down, not up. It was a windowless, square, cinder block building situated below the highway, which ran on a levee across long fields of soybeans and corn. The parking lot was level with the roof of the restaurant, and log steps with cinders between them led down to the door. Hickory smoke was pouring out of the square chimney and music out of the front door, which was propped open with a single concrete cowboy boot. The parking lot was filled with cars and pickups, most of them new. To the south, across the highway, new soybeans stretched off silvery-green in the light of the almost-full moon. To the north, behind the restaurant, a vast junkyard, the biggest Crystal had ever seen, filled the mile between the highway and the river. The Night Owl was separated from the junkyard by a chain link fence.

Williams followed Crystal down the log steps. People hung out around the door, smoking and drinking beer. Williams thought he saw a few familiar faces and nodded as they went in.

Behind a long counter, men in paper cowboy hats were turning slabs of mutton, Owensboro's specialty, over a hickory fire. Red leatherette booths were filled with people eating and drinking Cokes and beer. In a darker room in the back, a jukebox was playing and couples were dancing. Against the windowless wall facing the highway, young men were playing a row of video games.

There was no sign of Talking Man or of the woman in white. Williams looked in all the booths, and Crystal went to look in the back room.

"Hey, hoss," came a voice from near the video games. It was Hey Hoss Kost. Williams had gone to high school with him. Now he was a Deputy Sheriff. The girl with him was named Carol Ann. In high school, Williams had had a crush on her because she always looked scared, but she didn't look scared anymore. Hey Hoss had never looked scared.

"Hey." Williams nodded at them and started to follow Crystal toward the back room. Then, behind him, he heard a familiar sound—the scream of attacking missiles and the staccato, welcome stutter of defensive fire. Carol Ann was playing Missile Command. Williams stopped to watch. She was making a fatal mistake by being too protective of her left city; in Missile Command the only good defense is a good offense. Even as Williams watched, her center city was destroyed by alien fire. The explosion shook the room.

Williams looked around. Where had Crystal gone? The music had stopped in the back room and the lights were suddenly on. He heard running.

Crystal slipped between the wrecked cars as silently and swiftly as a moon shadow. She had to run to match the long strides of the man and woman she was following, but the ground was dry and soft, like leaves, and the going was easy.

She had seen them on the dance floor when she had gone into the back room. The woman was wearing a beaded sweater over her white dress and a scarf over her white hair. The man dancing with her was wearing a blue STP vest over a T-shirt and jeans. Crystal had never seen him before. The jukebox was playing Dickie Lee's "Nine Million, Nine Hundred Ninety-Nine Thousand, Nine Hundred Ninety-Nine Tears to Go." Crystal watched from the doorway as they danced toward their table. Still holding the woman by the waist, the man picked up a package wrapped in newspaper, then finished her beer and his, holding them both between his fingers in one hand like two cigarettes. The woman was wearing open-toed shoes, and Crystal could see that she had painted the ends of her toes red to hide the fact that she had no toenails.

The next song came on, and they danced toward the jukebox.

The jukebox was set against an unused door, blocking it. The man in the vest eased it away and reached behind it and turned the doorknob. Crystal could hear the lock snap across the room. The door opened a crack, and when she thought no one was looking, the woman slipped through, and the man followed her into the darkness. Crystal crossed the room. The door led outside into the junkyard. There was just enough room to squeeze between the wall and the jukebox, but Crystal made the mistake of trying to shut the door behind her. Something hit the jukebox and the record screeched. The lights came on inside, and she ran . . .

Now she was in the junkyard and the moon was full, making the shadows dark and huge. Ahead of her, she could see the man and woman, and she crossed over one lane so they wouldn't see her if they looked back.

The lanes between the wrecked cars were clear and wide like the streets of an abandoned city. The only trees were scrub locust and sassafras, adapted to grow through hoods, but the weeds grew in wild array. Pigweed and dock soared upward in fantastic formations; jungles of poke gathered in the low spots. Seeds from all over the world arrived at the junkyard clinging to bumpers and stuck in tire treads: jimsonweed and kudzu from the Deep South, buffalo grass from the high plains, raspberries and ramp from the mountains to the east, prairie flowers from the Texas roadsides, oriental vines that had clung to Toyotas, and grasses from the north of Italy and the south of France.

The thing in the package was a silver shotgun with a sawed-off stock and a sawed-off barrel. While he walked, the man unwrapped it and tossed the paper away. The woman took off her scarf, and her hair shone white and menacing.

Crystal wished Williams were with her. But if she went back to get him, she would lose them. Standing on her tiptoes, looking back, she could barely make out the roof of the Night Owl and the smoke from the barbecue fire.

The cars were all the same color in the moonlight. Ahead, there was a low rise. The man and the woman had stopped. Crystal crept up behind a '59 Barracuda to see what was going on. The man and the woman were also ducked down, sneaking up on something.

Then she saw what.

On the top of the rise, a dark '50 Ford four-door was slowly rising into the air. It hung for a moment like a balloon on a short string, five feet off the ground, then began slowly to turn over. Standing beside it, his feet spread apart and planted in the mud, and one hand in his jacket pocket, was Talking Man. Crystal was so glad to see him that she had to put her hands on her knees to stop herself from running up to him.

The Ford rotated slowly, then turned end for end, with taillights pointing up. It seemed to slip; the front settled down into the mud with the sound of glass breaking, but instead of falling over, it balanced there on its nose.

Talking Man pulled a ratchet from his pocket; Crystal recognized the ⅜-inch *Snap-On* driver he called his "Cadillac." Holding the car steady with one hand, he began to unfasten the oil pan, dropping the little ⁷⁄₁₆-inch bolts into the mud, junkman style.

To the side, behind a Buick V6, Crystal could see the man and woman watching as intently as she was.

Should she warn Talking Man?

They would shoot her. She knew that, with a certainty as cold as chrome. She sneaked up closer.

Talking Man had all the bolts out. He hit the oil pan with the side of his hand, and it popped off with a low musical sound. Black oil slopped out. He set it on the ground, then reached into the oil and pulled out a Mason jar. He wiped it clean with a rag from his pocket.

It was filled with a clear liquid like moonshine.

He lifted it up in the moonlight. It looked heavy. The stuff in it was rocking slowly back and forth like the sea. It pulled his arms back and forth.

The man and woman stood up.

Crystal shouted.

Talking Man ran down the back of the hill.

The Ford began to fall over.

Crystal screamed.

Yellow eyes. The man pointed the gun at her face. It was a double barrel.

Someone pushed her face first into the mud.

There was the sound of thunder or a gun.

Williams pushed Crystal face down into the mud, then dragged her behind an Oldsmobile. Behind him, he could hear glass breaking and feet sucking in mud. He couldn't tell if she was hit. He figured not, because he had felt the wind of the shotgun load go by. In the sky, fading now, he could see the glow that had led him back into the junkyard when he had looked behind the jukebox door.

"Wake up!" He leaned Crystal against the car and grabbed her cheeks and shook her face, but her eyes stayed closed tight. Keeping his head down, he looked through the dirty car windows. The woman in the white dress and the man in the STP vest were walking up the mound; the Ford lay on its roof, at the top, its glass all cracked. The man held the shotgun out in front of him with both hands like a long, coon-hunter's flashlight. The woman was carrying her sandals in one hand. Talking Man was nowhere to be seen.

The mound glittered in the moonlight—glass and mud.

"Wake up," Williams whispered, pinching Crystal's cheeks again.

Just then Williams heard a car start. It was an unusual sound in a junkyard late at night. It was unmistakably the Mustang. The deep-throated 351 Cleveland with the Memphis cam barked then growled behind the mound. Slipping in the soft dirt, the man and the woman started running toward the sound.

Williams started to follow them, but he couldn't wake Crystal up, and he didn't want to leave her.

Then, as the man and woman disappeared around

one side of the mound, the Mustang came around the other. The engine was racing and the car was drifting sideways in the mud. Talking Man was steering with the throttle as he tried to make a ninety-degree turn into a long row running west. It was too narrow. Williams winced. The Mustang kissed off the side of a Pontiac station wagon, spun halfway around, and settled into the mud.

Talking Man dropped it into reverse, and the wheels began to dig holes and climb out of them at the same time.

There was a boom and the left taillight disappeared.

The man and the woman ran around the side of the mound, high on the slope. There was a shot from inside the car and the man put his hand to his cheek then turned around, as if he'd thought of something awful. He dropped the shotgun, and the woman grabbed it before it tipped over into the mud.

There was a boom and the other taillight went out. The rear end of the Mustang danced left; the wheels found dirt, and the Mustang leaped forward.

There was a boom and the rear window exploded in the moonlight like a shower of stars.

"My God," Williams heard himself say.

The shotgun boomed once more, then boomed once more. Exhaust barking, lights out, the Mustang disappeared down the row. With the gun under one arm, the woman counted shells from her purse into her hand as she slid down the mound.

The man followed right behind her. For the first time, Williams noticed that he looked a little like Hey Hoss. He was holding the side of his face with one hand, and dark stuff was seeping out between his fingers. The man saw something on the ground and picked it up. It was a tie-rod end. He turned and looked back, and Williams realized that he and Crystal were standing in the open, between two rows of cars.

The man threw the tie-rod. Whirling like a bone, it missed Williams's head and shattered a Plymouth window behind him.

Pulling Crystal, Williams ran backward two rows. The moon was going behind bright, racy clouds. It was already full, but earlier that night it had only been a half. What was going on?

"Where's Talking Man?" Crystal asked calmly. She seemed still dazed.

"He got away and now they're after us."

Crystal stood up straight, and Williams stopped running. He could hear shots but now they were far away. He could see tears running down Crystal's face. The shots were like thunder, and the tears were like rain. Looking up, he was smacked in the face by two, three, four of those big, soft, cold, warm, marble-size, Ohio Valley raindrops, falling six inches apart.

Crystal opened the door of a nearby Cadillac and said, "Come on."

They got in out of the rain and went to sleep.

Crystal woke up leaning against Williams's shoulder. It was almost light, but gray. The rain drumming on the roof of the Cadillac sounded like the rain on the trailer roof at home. The seats smelled musty and safe. The shotgun blasts, the shouts, the breaking glass all seemed as far away as a dream, and when she closed her eyes again they went away perfectly.

10

WILLIAMS WOKE UP ONE eye at a time. Crystal's head was against his shoulder and her hair smelled like tobacco. It was the good smell, the smell of the great barns. It had stopped raining and it was getting light out.

Down the neck of her blouse, he could see her white bra with little blue flowers. It was loose, and he could see her nipple. He moved his head slightly . . . then suddenly something growled, and Crystal jumped and sat up.

"What was that!"

It was the ghost of the old power windows. Williams had leaned against the button. He pushed it, and the window rolled on down, then died. The morning air smelled good.

Crystal sat up. "Where are we?" She looked at the dashboard of the Cadillac, then looked at Williams, then remembered. She reached for a cigarette, but her purse was gone.

Williams got out of the car to pee, then sat on the hood. Crystal peed behind the big fins, then joined him. She smoked a butt she found in the ashtray. Neither of them wanted to talk about the fighting the night before. Like a dream left unremembered, it might still go away. But they had to find her purse.

The junkyard looked different in the innocence of day. The cars were shiny from last night's rain.

They crossed over two rows, picking their way between the new puddles. Williams wasn't surprised to see the mound with the '50 Ford, resting on its roof, slid halfway down the side. The oil pan was off; the crankshaft was gnarled and dark like a dinosaur bone. He wasn't even surprised to see the red-and-blue plastic shotgun shells scattered down the slope, or the spray of glass where the Mustang had been hit. He had never believed, even for a second, that it had really only been a dream.

They searched around the Oldsmobile where they had hidden and between the rows where they had run, but no purse.

Two rows over, they found the Mustang.

"I'm sorry," Crystal said.

Williams didn't say anything.

He walked slowly around it. There were holes in the fenders. There were holes in the doors. The tires were all flat. The glass was all gone. Even the dials on the dashboard had been shot away. The hood was sprung open, and the carburetor had been blown off the manifold at close range. Williams groaned and closed his eyes. He opened them again. It was exactly the same. The Mustang had been shot to pieces.

"I'm sorry," Crystal said again. She reached for his hand, but he pulled it away. There was no sign of Talking Man, but no blood on the seat either. At least he had gotten away. Maybe.

"I just thought of something," Crystal said.

"What?"

"What if the Chrysler is gone, too?"

She started walking toward the Night Owl as fast as she could go. Williams followed, but he wasn't in such a hurry. It didn't matter to him. He was in enough trouble as it was.

The jukebox door was closed and locked, so Crystal and Williams squeezed through the space between the chain link fence and the concrete block wall of the Night Owl. They climbed the bank to the parking lot. It was almost empty except for the Chrysler. At the other end of the lot, two men stood by a blue Daviess County sheriff's cruiser. They looked up when Crystal and Williams came up the bank, but went on talking.

Williams was about to unlock the Chrysler when a voice said in a loud whisper, "Hey girl!"

Down the log steps, in the door of the Night Owl, a woman in a waitress dress was holding a big purse.

"Your daddy left this for you, honey."

"Thank you."

The woman looked at the blue cruiser. "I think he's in a world of trouble," she said. "I think he stole Hey Hoss's truck last night."

"Are you a friend of his?" Crystal asked.

"No, I've just seen him around. He just told me to give you this. He didn't even say your name . . ."

"Hit's Crystal."

"Let me ask you this," Williams said. "Did he actually talk to you? What did he say exactly?"

The woman looked confused, then suspicious. "It was busy, and I don't remember his exact words."

She did remember exactly, and that was the problem. The man had talked to her without words. The man had looked her in the eye, handed her the purse, and put pictures in her mind of a baby girl growing into a young daughter, a picture of a whole life in one second, and then he had walked out the door in a big hurry. The woman even knew what Crystal's room in the trailer looked like. Her name was Rose and this was the second time this had happened to her, the first being the time when the preacher at Little Creek had held her two hands and made her see her baby boy being killed in a car wreck and rising up toward heaven before he was even born.

But she wasn't about to tell these two that.

"Be careful, honey," she said to the girl who lived in the trailer.

The Chrysler was already hot from the sun. The two men walked over as soon as they saw Williams start unlocking the door. It was Hey Hoss and the sheriff.

"Somebody stole my truck last night," Hey Hoss said.

"I just heard that," Williams said.

"Are you sorry to hear it?"

"What the hell do you mean by that?" Williams looked from Hey Hoss to the sheriff, who was fishing with two fingers in a pouch of Red Man.

"It was an old guy in a floppy hat, some hillbilly-looking son of a bitch," Hey Hoss said.

"So what does that have to do with me?"

Williams looked back at the sheriff, who looked totally uninterested. This worried him, because when cops get bored there's no telling what they'll do. He opened the door on the passenger side of the Chrysler, and Crystal got in. Walking smoothly, as if he were walking around snakes, he walked around to the driver side.

"Got papers on this car, son?" the sheriff asked.

"It's not my car," Williams said. He forced himself to talk real slow. "But then it's not your truck either," he said to Hey Hoss.

"Whose car might it be?" the sheriff asked.

"Hit's mine."

Crystal had opened the purse. She pulled out a wad of paper wrapped around a lump that, as she unwrapped it, proved to be the little owl from the top of the TV.

The papers were damp. One was a roadmap and the other was a registration. Crystal smoothed out the registration and handed it to the sheriff.

"You're Jean Pore-Bay-Less?"

She nodded.

"From Alley Row-Jay, New Mexico?"

"Hit's my mother's car."

"You're a long way from home. What were you all doing in the junkyard all night?"

"Fooling around," Williams said.

"Don't give me no fooling around."

"Sorry."

"You're Junior Williams's boy, aren't you?"

"Yes, sir."

The sheriff handed the papers back to Crystal, who wrapped them back around the owl and stuck them into the glove compartment.

"Don't be fooling around here no more."

Williams turned the key. The Chrysler caught on the first hit.

"Look, I'm sorry about your truck, Hey Hoss. But you've got no business thinking I took it."

"Did I say you took it? Did I?"

Hey Hoss glared at him. The conversation seemed to be over. Williams backed out and pulled onto the highway, heading back into town.

"I'm glad you had those papers in your purse," Williams said.

"Except hit's not my purse. Mine was a Knoxville World's Fair purse. I've never seen this one before in my life."

As they drove into town Crystal smoothed the map across her knees. Owensboro was, as on most maps, near the center. Far to the west and south there was a circle drawn in pencil around a Spanish name near the Mexico border. Written next to it was "Meet Me Here."

"Allah Row-Jay," Crystal read.

Williams, who'd had Spanish in high school, corrected her. "Ala Roja. It means Red Wing. What else is there?"

"This." She held up the owl. Williams reached for it, but she pulled it away. "And these." She held up five .30-30 cartridges.

"Don't hold them up," Williams said. "Look behind us without being obvious."

Crystal fixed her lipstick in the rearview mirror. The

sheriff and Hey Hoss were following in the blue cruiser.

They drove east through town and south on Livermore Road. The blue cruiser followed. They drove north, winding through the new subdivisions south of the south side. The blue cruiser followed. Williams stopped at a 7-Eleven so Crystal could get cigarettes, and the blue cruiser parked on the street a half a block away; they shut off the cruiser when Crystal got out of the car and started it again as soon as she got back in. Williams drove north across Ford Avenue and down toward Parrish, then back up Cottage Drive and back down Robin Road. Every time he turned a corner, he put the gas to the floor as soon as the blue cruiser was out of sight; but every time he braked for the next corner, there it was, always a little less than a block behind.

"Maybe they think we're going to lead them to the truck," Crystal said.

"Maybe."

Williams drove through a shopping center lot and a drive-in cleaners and even under the entrance canopy at the Executive Inn. Still, the blue cruiser followed. He did everything but go the wrong way on a one-way street, because all they had to do then was turn on the siren and arrest him. Then he got an idea. He drove out Frederica, past the world's largest sassafras tree, then circled back to his parents' house.

His father's Buick was gone, as usual, but his mother's Ford was parked in the driveway.

He pulled in behind it.

The blue cruiser parked a half a block down the street.

"What is this place?" Crystal asked.

"My parents' house. I'm going to go in for a minute. I'm leaving the keys in the car. Watch for my signal."

He got out of the car; the cruiser, a half a block away, shut off its engine.

The side door was unlocked, as usual. Williams opened the refrigerator and took a swig of milk. Upstairs, he could see the flickering light of the TV. He went up. His mother was asleep under a rose-colored bedspread. Everything in the bedroom was blue and rose except for the TV.

"Hi, Mom."

Of course, she didn't answer.

"Just picking up a few things."

He opened his father's dresser drawer.

"School's going great. I have to hurry back and study, actually."

Under the socks, there was an old wallet with gas company credit cards that his father used only on trips. Williams shuffled through the cards and decided on the Mobil. He looked for money but there wasn't any.

"Well, bye now."

He kissed his mother on the cheek and looked out through the curtains. Hey Hoss and the sheriff were sitting in the blue cruiser, leaning back, smoking cigarettes, waiting for him to come out the side door.

He went downstairs and climbed out the kitchen window into the back yard. Standing behind the house where Crystal could see him but they couldn't, he signaled to her: With his thumb and forefinger he made a motion like turning a key.

He had forgotten to tell her to stay out of the driver's seat so they wouldn't start the cruiser. But Crystal was smart. She slid over far enough to fix her lipstick in the rearview mirror, and while she was leaning forward looking at herself, the Chrysler started almost soundlessly.

Come this way, Williams motioned.

Crystal reached down for what seemed to be a comb. With no one in the driver's seat, the Chrysler suddenly leaped forward and around the Ford in the driveway, kissing bumpers gently as it turned into the soft grass and around into the back yard.

Williams could hear the cruiser start up out on the street. The Chrysler skidded to a stop, and he jumped into the driver's seat. Crystal pulled her feet off the pedals just as his hit, and the car leaped forward again, spraying grass and sod across the back of the house. Williams slipped the Chrysler between two maples, crushed a small flowered border, and pulled through the neighbors's yard, flashing past Mrs. Waltrip's alarmed face in her kitchen window. Far behind, through the driveway, Crystal could see the blue cruiser just getting into gear.

Williams pulled out of the Waltrip's yard onto Cottage Drive in a four-wheel drift with the old dry-rotted tires screaming, hitting 65 by the end of the block. Taking a chance, he ran the stop sign and cut through the back lot of a tobacco warehouse on Parrish, then out onto Locust. There he slowed down. There was nobody following. Worried about a radio call, he headed straight out Ninth and then Crabtree into the small clay hills west of Owensboro. He followed a one-lane dirt road and hit Highway 60 just past Deemer's Dairy Drive-In.

"Good going," Crystal said.

"Same to you," Williams grinned. The Chrysler loved running fast; he ran it out smoothly up to 60, 70,

80. The highway was clear behind. "Spread that map out," he said. "What's that town your daddy marked?"

Crystal spread the map out on her knees. "Red Bird."

"Red Wing. What does it say?"

"It says 'Meet Me Here.'"

"Well, let's go."

"What do you mean?"

"I might as well go with you."

"Really?" She grinned without meaning to.

"I guess so. I can't go back to Bowling Green. And now I can't go back to Owensboro either."

"Suit yourself," Crystal said. Secretly, she was pleased. At least two of them might have a chance. She put her head out the window and bathed her face in the cool, warm, rushing-by highway summer time air.

11

HIGHWAY 60 FOLLOWS THE Ohio River but never acknowledges it. Where the river runs straight, the highway turns, twisting between the low hills and through the hollows. Where the river bends, it runs straight, cutting off the ends of the long bottoms, ignoring the huge loops of river the centuries drew. From the highway, the river is hardly ever seen: only an occasional muddy flash through the trees that's gone like a dream almost but not quite remembered.

The trees were now green: fully dressed, Crystal thought, since this trouble had started. The end of spring had ended and the beginning of summer had begun. The tobacco plants in the fields were standing up after lying on the ground for their first week, deliberately, she had always figured, to scare their owners into taking good care of them. She thought of her own field, disked and ready for the plants that were crammed shoulder to shoulder in a box in the back of a hot old pickup, probably dying. Would they die before she found Talking Man and returned to set them? It didn't do any good to worry, so she quit worrying as the Chrysler sped west.

Near Spottsville, they crossed the Green River again, where it empties its deep, cavey water into the Ohio. Near the road, a family was following a tractor across a hillside, setting their tobacco late. Williams looked across at Crystal, but she hardly seemed to notice.

The Chrysler sailed along smoothly at 70, 75. Williams knew the road between Owensboro and Henderson by heart. His grandmother had seen these bottomlands from one side only, the river side, riding the Gayoso from Evansville up the Green; there had still been bears then, scratching their rear ends on the fallen logs. Williams's mother had seen the country from both sides. Williams knew it only from the highway side. As a child, he had ridden Highway 60 a thousand times with his chin on the rear window deck, watching the world rush away, the ditches and tall weeds the fastest, the faraway barns more slowly, like wooden ships.

Now here he was, going to New Mexico.

It was dark by the time they got to Paducah. Kids sat on the hoods of their cars at the Dairy Queen and watched them pass, the only car on the highway. There was no sign of the pickup Talking Man was supposed to have stolen, and no sign of the white mystery car.

"Do you know what the pickup looks like?" Crystal asked.

"It's a blue '72 Dodge with upright pipes and mag wheels. It's kind of unmissable."

"Do you mean to catch up with him before we get to Red Man?"

"Red Wing. Maybe. I thought I would try."

"Because he drives really fast. I don't think you can catch up with him."

"I don't know about that," Williams said, insulted. "Anyway, we need gas."

They filled the Chrysler at a Mobil station. Crystal needed cigarettes, but the attendant wouldn't put them on the card. There was also the problem of food. The attendant wouldn't put even a candy bar on the card. "Only gas and oil products," he said, a teenager in a Purolater hat, enjoying his power.

There was a special on Valvoline, and Williams bought a case for $16.95 and put it on the card. Then he drove back to the Dairy Queen. He pulled in beside a car that didn't look like it was borrowed from Dad: a copper-colored '65 Plymouth Barracuda with phony lake pipes. A couple sat on the hood. The boy had shoulder-length blond hair and the girl had wide blue eyes that looked to Crystal like they had rolled out of a set of doll dishes.

"Want to buy a case of oil?"

"Naw."

After some dickering they got seven dollars. Williams and Crystal each had a small burger, and at the 7-Eleven they bought two packs of Marlboros, one Big Gulp and a bag of potato chips to share, a Snickers and a Clark Bar for later, and headed west. It was almost midnight.

* * *

West of Paducah begins Kentucky's Deep South, where the Mississippi delta extends its long finger its farthest north, even to the tip of Illinois at Cairo. There is an occasional cotton field alternated with the soybeans, a few loblolly pines among the maples and hickories, cypress in the bayous along the Tennessee line, and the roadsides are dark, dark green with kudzu.

The highway here was flat and straight, shining dull white in the moonlight; it was an old concrete slab of the type Williams's uncle Sam had made a fortune building after the war. The road followed the river, always angling south and west, but Williams couldn't see the river, not even on the turns, because since they had left Paducah the road never got high enough. About fifty miles west of Paducah, he saw a mountain to the north, on the Illinois side. This was a surprise, since he knew there were no mountains in Illinois. As a kid Williams had dreamed over the "Mountains" section in the *World Book*, fascinated, as only a child from the bottomlands can be, by the pictures of Colorado and Tibet, Switzerland and North Carolina. Even Pennsylvania, with its long folded ridges, had made him envy kids who grew up where they could look up and see something besides sky. Williams knew that there were no mountains or even big hills in western Kentucky or southern Illinois. But there it was—long and black with timber, looming against the midnight sky.

It was no bank of clouds. Williams could see a mercury vapor light far up the side and headlights working their way down a switchback on the steep south slope. At the west end, a white cliff gleamed like bone.

Williams puzzled over the mountain until it fell behind, out of sight. He wanted to point it out to Crystal, but she was asleep with the map and the owl on her lap.

Driving at night with no radio gets boring. Williams pulled off the highway to sleep on a dirt road just past a sign that read: MISSISSIPPI TOLL BRIDGE 5 MILES. The road followed a deep ditch between two soybean fields. He drove until he was out of sight of the highway and stopped. There were no houses visible, nothing but beans and trees in the distance. There was no way to know what time it was. In the middle of the soybeans, an old tobacco barn, with gaps in its boards like a wrecked ship, gleamed in the moonlight.

Williams went to sleep dreaming about mountains for the first time since he was a kid. Crystal was awake, but she kept her eyes closed until his breathing told her he was asleep. Then she sat on the hood and smoked her last cigarette. The moon looked bigger than it ought to, she thought, and she could see clouds on it. She held the owl, trying to warm it between her hands. She missed Talking Man.

When Williams woke up, the door was open on Crystal's side and she was gone. Her purse and her shoes were on the seat, though, and he could hear her splashing down in the ditch. She had left the door open and the dome light was on. Williams only wanted to nudge the starter to check the battery, but as soon as he turned the key, the Chrysler started right up.

"Hey!"

Crystal ran up the bank from the ditch with a worried look on her face. She was carrying her white cotton pullover blouse in one hand and her socks in the other, wearing only her jeans and her white bra with little blue flowers.

"I'm not going anywhere," Williams said. "I was just checking the battery. I didn't mean to start the car."

"Well, how am I to know," she said angrily, turning her back and pulling the blouse over her head. "And I help you goat sure elms fools."

"What?"

"I hope you got your eyes full."

Williams blushed. He had.

There was no room to turn around, so Williams backed out to the highway. Something was different, he could feel it before he could see it. Last night they had pulled off a deserted highway, but this morning the road was jammed with cars and pickups, none of them moving. At first Williams thought there had been a wreck, but as he waited for someone to let him out onto the highway, he could see that the line stretched as far as he could see in both directions, all headed west, toward the Mississippi River Toll Bridge.

12

AN OLD MAN IN a rusted-out Dodge station wagon let the Chrysler in behind a Ford pickup with South Missouri plates.

The line of cars moved slower than a walk. No one seemed impatient. No horns honked. Some people walked ahead to visit with people in other cars; others just sat and stared or smoked as the line inched forward, stopping, then starting, then stopping.

"What the hell is South Missouri?" Williams wondered out loud. Crystal looked at him blankly. The question seemed silly to Williams as soon as he heard himself ask it. It was the state across the river.

Crystal walked ahead to bum a cigarette from two teenage boys sitting with a hound in the back of the Ford pickup.

"How far is the nearest store?" she asked.

"Up top of the hill."

"How come the traffic is so bad?"

"Hit's the bridge. Hit's always like this."

The line moved on slowly. Williams tried the radio again, but it still didn't work. He could hear the radios from the other cars, all on the same station apparently, playing "Satin Sheets" by Jeannie Pruitt. But it was too dim to enjoy listening to.

Crystal found one more long butt and then bummed another from the boys in the truck. They were working the dog, throwing a corncob into the soybean field, which he returned soggy with spit. Crystal didn't see how they could stand to pick it up to throw it again. Every time the dog brought it back it, he crashed stupidly into the side of the truck.

By midmorning they were at the bottom of the hill, and Crystal could see the white frame store through the trees, a hundred yards away at the top.

"I'm going to walk up to the store and get me some cigarettes," she said.

"Let me go," Williams said.

He stepped out while the car was moving and Crystal slid behind the wheel. She didn't mind. "Marlboros," she said.

As he walked past the cars up the hill, Williams said "howdy" to all the drivers. It was a friendly crowd. No one seemed bothered by the delay. There was a fire burning in a drum in the back of one pickup, and people were frying fish. In other cars, people were asleep. Most of the plates were from Kentucky and South Missouri, with a few from Illinois.

As he climbed higher Williams looked back. The line

of cars stretched across the wide soybean field and over the next hill. Beyond the hill, east and slightly north, he could see the blue line of Pennyrile Mountain. Almost 4,000-feet high, it dominated all of southern Illinois and western Kentucky. He remembered going there as a kid with his parents to see the long, narrow "Lake of the Clouds" that lay in a fold along the mile-long summit. Every time Williams saw the mountain he remembered how disappointed he'd been to find just a plain water lake and no clouds at all.

The store was called Gormsley's Grocery. The outside was white shingles covered with soft-drink signs from the distant past. The inside looked just like any other country store in the Upper Mid South: candy, tobacco seed, cotton gloves, flashlight batteries, calendars, twine.

The parking lot was empty, but the store was filled with people who, like Williams, had walked in without pulling their cars out of line.

The soft-drink machine was the old-fashioned type, where the bottles are trapped under a cage of bars and have to be snaked out and then pulled up through a coin-operated gate. Most of the drinks were unfamiliar, but Williams managed to find two Dr. Peppers and get them out. He opened them and got in line to buy the cigarettes and some candy bars.

Behind the counter, there was an old woman in a white dress wearing a green plastic visor that said "Lake of the Clouds." Behind her, a fat man in khaki pants sat on a milk crate wearing a pistol and holding a shotgun across his lap. It was odd to see guns in a store except during dove or squirrel season. Pinned to the wall above the man's head, a printed sign said: THESE PREMISES PROTECTED BY AN ARMED AMERICAN.

"Two packs of Marlboros, two bags of potato chips, and two Snickers, please," Williams said when he got to the counter.

The woman handed him the potato chips and the cigarettes. "Scissors?" she asked.

"Snickers."

"Never heard of it," the woman said.

"Snickers. Candy bars."

"She said she never heard of it," the man with the guns said.

Williams tried to think of what else Crystal might like. "How about a Clark Bar?"

The woman shook her head. The man shook his head behind her. The shotgun looked like a metal cat awake across his knees.

"A Reese Cup? A Hershey with almonds? A Mars Bar? A Payday?"

The old woman shook her head. "I never heard of none of them," she said, pointing into the case. Williams looked down. There were candy bars arranged in neat little boxes, but they all looked strange. Golden Boy. Collie Bar. A round chocolate thing called a Whilliker. They looked close but not right.

"How about a Nestle's Crunch?" Williams asked. But that didn't sound right even to him. "How about a Baby Ruth?"

"Watch your mouth," the man said.

Williams looked up at the cigarettes. Camels. Marlboros. They looked just as weird as the candy bars when he looked at them long enough.

"What's the holdup?" someone asked from back in the line.

"Two Collie Bars," Williams said.

He paid and walked out into the sun. The line of

cars was moving faster, and the Chrysler was just passing the store. Williams got in on the passenger side and gave Crystal her Marlboros.

"I was afraid I would pass the store before you got out," she said. "What took so long?"

"I don't know. It was weird in there. There was a huge line. Here, I got us something to eat."

"Oh boy," Crystal said. "A Collie Bar."

Just then, they crossed the top of the hill and the road came out of the trees. There, far below, deep in its red-walled canyon, was the world-famous northward-flowing, catfish-colored Mississippi River.

13

CRYSTAL DROVE THE FIRST half mile down the narrow one-lane switchback. The river lay far below at the bottom of a canyon six miles wide and a thousand feet deep. The Kentucky side was barren and treeless and kept that way by mud slides. The South Missouri side was too far away to see clearly, but its color suggested it was the same.

The road was bare dirt, powdery from thousands of tires, switching back on itself in 170-degree turns every quarter of a mile. Driving it reminded Crystal of working a field with the John Deere, turning at the end of each row—brake, turn, throttle—except that instead of pulling a disk she was bumper to bumper with a pickup in front and a station wagon in back; and coming out of every turn the front end of the Chrysler hung out heart-stoppingly over a thousand-foot drop as smooth and steep as the side of a tent.

Going off the road on every turn were the tire marks of cars that hadn't made it.

The river far below was fast and muddy and almost two miles wide. There were three bridges. The road was directly under the highest and grandest of them, a suspension bridge that soared off the top of the bluff, angling upward and out for four miles before it was sliced off exactly in the middle—where the cables met the roadway—some said by a meteor, some said by a bomb. On the South Missouri side, the tower had fallen, and it lay on the canyon floor with its half of the bridge, twisted and dark with rust. The half that was supported from the Kentucky tower still held, the roadway holding the cables out and the cables holding the roadway up. Although no wind was stirring in the canyon, high above, at the end of the bridge, a 200-foot dangling piece of concrete slab, with a car wedged between it and a cable, was making slow circles in the wind.

The second bridge was far below at the bottom of the canyon. It was concrete and had fallen all in one piece. Parts of it lay in the shallow water and parts lay on the bank, cracked and flat like a cake that had been dropped.

The third bridge, the one the traffic was snaking across, lay directly on top of the water. It was made out of pieces of the other two, plus barges and billboards, roof tin and random junk. It was bowed northward with the current and covered with a slowly moving line of cars.

The six-mile-long line of cars was the only color in the landscape, the only thing moving except for the bridge end high above. The line inched downward, back and forth on long, steep switchbacks, and then west across the river on the pieced-together bridge. On the other side, it split into two streams: one heading north on a four-lane that angled up through a cut in the bank; the other heading up the canyon wall on a switchback like the one they were descending on the Kentucky side. Both were filled with cars.

Though the Chrysler was still high on the bluff, Williams could smell the muddy water. At wide spots on the bridge, he could see tiny figures with come-alongs winching in house-size catfish caught in chain-link nets. He remembered reading about them, though he couldn't remember in what magazine. Once thought to be rare, these 1,700-year-old monsters were becoming more common as the river dropped and the pools that sheltered them became exposed.

"I think I see him," Williams said.

"Huh?" Crystal had been sleeping, dozing with her head against the door. They were almost at the bottom of the Kentucky bank.

"Talking Man. I saw him on the bridge in the pickup."

Crystal sat up. It was almost dark, and the cars were hardly moving at all. Three feet. Stop. Fifteen feet. Stop. Ten feet. Stop. When she had gone to sleep, it had been late afternoon, and they had been halfway down the switchback. Now they were almost at the bottom, but the river was still over a mile away.

"How can you see anything that far away? It's too dark."

"It's a thing I noticed in Owensboro. I can see him if I don't look exactly at him."

Williams had discovered this ability back at the Night Owl, when he had slipped through the jukebox door after hearing all the commotion and seeing it open. He had been looking for Crystal, not Talking Man. It was dark in the junkyard, but he had seen, out of the corner of his eye, the Ford spinning in the air and Talking Man standing beside it, one hand in his pocket.

When he had tried to look directly toward him, he had seen nothing but dark rows of cars. But looking away, he could walk toward him. He could see him clearly, like in a telescope. He could even see Crystal, watching.

This time, he had been watching a fire on the South Missouri bank near the bridge. Tiny figures were cutting up a giant hump of catfish as big as a car. They were too far away to see clearly, but while watching them, from the corner of his eye Williams saw Talking Man step out of a pickup onto the wet billboards of the bridge, light a cigarette, shake his arms out, stretch, get back in. The truck was a blue Dodge four-by-four with upright stacks and chrome wheels—Hey Hoss's, no doubt about it. Talking Man was a car thief.

Then Williams tried to look at him, and he was gone. Williams tried looking at the fire again, then looked upstream, but he couldn't connect again.

"Look away again," Crystal suggested.

But it didn't do any good. Williams searched the line of cars directly for the Dodge, but the colors got lost in the distance and the dusk before the cars even reached the bridge, still a mile away. It was growing darker and car lights were coming on. On the banks of the river, more fires were appearing.

"At least we know he's there," Crystal said.

Near the bottom of the switchback, the road widened. On an impulse, Williams pulled out to pass. The rear end of the Chrysler slipped downhill in the soft clay, then spun and held. They passed one car, then another, before the road narrowed and forced the Chrysler back in.

"I'm going to catch him," Williams said.

It was slow going, but it was less boring than sitting behind the same car or truck for hours. People didn't seem to mind being passed. Families slept in the backs of pickups under corrugated fiberglass roofs. One old man was carrying hogs to market in a Cadillac with the rear doors removed so they could jump in and out to graze on the scarce grass. Behind, to the east, the high canyon wall loomed dark with car lights strung down it, white and red, like Christmas tree lights.

Crystal kept count with lipstick marks on the rearview mirror. By the time they reached the broken slabs of the bridge approach, they were fourteen cars ahead of where they had been; but how far behind Talking Man, they had no way of knowing.

14

THE BRIDGE WAS WIDER than the road but crowded with wrecked cars and, in some places, shacks. Mothers hung out in the doorways, while their kids ran up and down selling food to the passing cars. It was no easier to pass on the bridge, but it was more complicated, as they could sometimes pass on one side and sometimes on the other. On the switchback it had always been on the left facing north and on the right facing south.

Crystal drove for an hour, but Williams couldn't sleep, so she let him drive again. She never had trouble sleeping.

The air was cool and fishy-smelling down here, on the water. Williams found fewer and fewer chances to pass. Leaning his head out the window, he could see the half bridge far overhead, pointing like a great finger west. It bothered him because he remembered it, but he couldn't remember what he remembered about it. He had the feeling that as they traveled west the world was changing, but as it changed, his memories changed too, so that he couldn't tell what had changed and what hadn't. For example, he remembered something weird about the candy bars back at the store, but he couldn't remember now what was weird about them. The bridge looked familiar, and he remembered being a kid watching it out of the back window of a car, crossing over it, or under it . . . or was that a memory he had made up?

He unwrapped the last Collie Bar and quit worrying about it. Whatever was weird about the candy bars, it wasn't the familiar picture of the dog looking up faithfully.

Crystal was asleep when they crossed the higher, middle section of the bridge, rattling the tin sheets. Suddenly the radio came on, and Williams wondered if maybe it was picking up signals from the half bridge a thousand feet overhead. The only station he could get was WKLY from Wheeling, Virginia. It came and went, came and went, as the Chrysler stopped and started and Crystal tossed and turned on the seat. Williams kept it low so she could sleep. Country music makes people who have never even left home homesick—and here he was heading for Mexico, almost. He didn't feel any more or less homesick than usual, but he passed up two chances to pass because there was something peaceful about inching forward on the slippery logs in the cool headlight light, listening to the tick of idling engines, the faraway radio steel guitars, the slap of muddy water on wood, the creaking of telephone pole timbers.

It was midnight.

He bought some fish and cracklings from a woman who was cooking over a fifty-five-gallon drum stove by the roadway; he bought watery coffee from her daughter and two Tropicana cartons of gas from her son, who poured it in through a paper funnel between moves. That was his last five-dollar bill.

He couldn't see the moon behind the high bluffs, but he could see its shine on the bridge above.

He passed a pickup on blocks with a fire in the bed and a fiddle player on the roof, all but his boots lost in the shadows. Two couples were slow dancing. A boy went car to car collecting coins. Seeing his Golden Grain hat, Williams realized they were out of the burley belt, into the corn belt.

It was getting lighter.

Williams pulled out to pass a Studebaker with a barking dog in the opened trunk, and the radio went off as Crystal sat up and looked around.

"I've been asleep," she said, as if explaining something to herself.

There was a flash of light high overhead. It was the still-invisible arriving sunrise hitting the glass of the wrecked car dangling from the half bridge. Crystal straightened and lighted a cigarette and looked around. The dawn was racing down the South Missouri bluff ahead of them, flashing on the cars on the switchback one by one like a video game coming on.

High above, the half bridge gleamed like a jeweled belt. Above it, gleamed clouds.

There were twenty-two marks on the rearview mirror. Crystal was driving while Williams tried unsuccessfully looking at the sky, the ground, even the cars behind. He had to find Talking Man again, before the road split between the four-lane heading north and the switchback heading west up the bluff. Otherwise, how would they know which way he had gone?

Crystal passed a Chevy van, and Williams put a mark on the mirror. They were off the bridge now, on the log and billboard road leading to the foot of the bluff, but it was no easier to pass. The road was narrow, and cars were bogged down to their axles in the mud on both sides.

At a wide spot there was a fire, and Crystal bought fried fish with fifty cents she found under the seat. Williams was sick of fish. On the riverbank, he could see men in rubber boots climbing over a giant, still-shaking body with six-foot knives.

He was beginning to worry about gas.

Crystal was beginning to worry about money.

Williams fiddled with the radio, but it had given up the ghost completely. Maybe, like most radios, it liked night best. They passed a Dodge Dart. Williams put another mark on the mirror.

They were only a few cars from where the road split and they still didn't know which way Talking Man had gone.

They passed a '68 Buick, an old Pontiac, . . . and then a white car with a white-haired woman driving. It was her. Now she had two men with her.

The man in the STP vest who looked like Hey Hoss was sitting beside her holding a shotgun upright. In the back seat was a smaller man with a rat mustache wearing a cowboy hat. To Williams's surprise, he looked a little like Hey Hoss, too. He was waving a Buck knife with one hand and rolling the window down with the other, grinning at Crystal then Williams then Crystal, as if he couldn't decide who to start cutting up first. The woman's eyes looked right into Crystal's as Crystal hit the gas, throwing the Chrysler sideways and then up the switchback fork.

The mystery car followed.

"Why did you slow down?"

"I didn't."

"Well, you're going slower."

"If you're so smart, why don't you drive?"

Williams looked back. The white car was following with one wheel on the road and one in the mud. The cowboy was waving the knife out the window. "All right, I will."

Crystal lifted off the seat, and Williams slid under her.

"How come you went this way?" he asked.

"I don't know. Where did they come from anyway? I didn't see them until hit was too late."

"I guess they were following Talking Man."

"Now they're following us. Was that your friend with them?"

"It looked a little like him. But they both did. Anyway, he's no friend of mine."

There were no more places to pass as the line climbed the switchback. It moved faster than on the Kentucky side, but it was still slow—3, 4, 5 miles per hour. Eight cars behind, Williams could see the mysterious white car. He started looking for a place to pass. He didn't find it until they were on the highest leg of the switchback, a thousand feet above the Mississippi.

Far below, the river gleamed in the afternoon light. The fires were being lit again. The half bridge was tangled in clouds, and the hanging beams swung through the mist like knives cutting biscuit flour.

Williams approached the sharp left turn that began the last and highest leg of the switchback. With a little wheel-spinning, he had managed to pass one car on every turn—six in all so far—but the mystery car had managed to do the same. It was still eight cars behind.

Nine, Williams thought, as he squeezed between the bluff wall and a Dodge station wagon.

The road here was narrow, but there was a smooth sloping shoulder a half a car wide on the outside, between the road and the thousand-foot drop.

"Here they come," Crystal said. "Eight again."

Williams decided to try it.

He eased out to the left into nothingness. When he felt his rear wheels start to slip, he hit the gas until they caught and spun the wheel right. The Chrysler was drifting forward almost sideways with the rear end downhill and the headlights pointed up at the sky.

Crystal started looking for a cigarette. It felt like they were falling.

Williams danced with the gas pedal: If he slowed, they would slip down; too much power, and they would straighten and roll over backward off the bluff. In the rearview mirror, he could see the river, a thousand feet below, behind the lipstick marks.

"They're trying hit," Crystal said.

Williams kept one foot on the gas and one hand on the wheel, using the two together like wings, his right front tire barely on the road, his left rear spinning in the clay. He worried about the gas, because if the Chrysler missed even one lick they were dead.

"They're still coming," Crystal said. "They're hanging on with one wheel. Uh oh, do we look that bad?"

They were almost at the top. Williams passed a Chevy pickup and then scraped an Olds station wagon, but not enough to slow him down. The three men in the Olds looked angry. Tough luck, thought Williams. He was home free. There was nothing between him and the end of the road, where it disappeared over the top of the bluff.

He drifted the Chrysler back onto the road. When the left rear wheel hit the harder dirt of the road, he flew forward like a stone from a slingshot.

"They're coming around the Olds now," Crystal said. "But the Olds is squeezing them over. Now they're slipping back, spinning their wheels. Uh oh, too slow. They're slipping back . . ."

Williams could see weeds waving ahead.

"Now their both front wheels are off the ground. They're slipping back. Their front end is picking up. I can see their tie-rods. Uh oh."

Williams eased over the crest of the bluff, his muffler scraping slightly. Surprisingly, the road ended in a field of hay; beyond it was an interstate with no cars on it.

"They turned over," Crystal said, horrified and pleased.

The Chrysler made a whispery sound speeding across the grass.

15

THE RADIO ONLY PLAYED when Crystal was asleep. It went off again every time she woke up.

Williams figured it out after they found a hole in the fence and got on the highway, heading south and west. The Chrysler stretched her long legs: 65, 75, 85. There were no other cars on the highway, coming or going. Crystal wiped the lipstick off the rearview mirror with warm Coke and Kleenex, finished her cigarette, and lay down on the seat.

Seconds after she closed her eyes, the radio came on. She sat up, startled. "Where are they?"

"We lost them, remember?" Williams patted her hand. The radio had gone off. "They went over backward. They're dead." He fiddled with the dial while she lay back down and closed her eyes. The radio came on again, louder, because he had turned it up.

Crystal sat up. "What was that?"

It was off again.

"Nothing," Williams said. "Go to sleep." It was like somebody waking themselves up with their own snoring. He thought about telling her but decided not to. She and Talking Man had enough secrets; he needed a few.

He turned it way down and turned it up slowly after she had gone to sleep.

At first the countryside was rolling, with grass on the hilltops and trees down in the draws, mostly little oaks. There were no plowed fields and the few farmhouses were small, with small barns. It was like a stretched-out Ohio County with one-third of the trees. Sometimes, in the distance, on county roads off the interstate, Williams could see a truck or car, but there was no traffic on the highway. The road was in good shape, but the entrances and the exits were blocked with yellow fifty-five-gallon drums.

Since they didn't pass any cars, Williams figured that the cars that had climbed the bluff before them had turned north or perhaps turned off at the first exit, a north-south interstate for LITTLE ROCK and ST. LOUIS that hadn't been blocked by the yellow drums.

There was no sign of Talking Man.

Across the median, heading north and east, he saw traffic twice. Once they passed a military convoy of mustard-yellow trucks filled with men sitting up sleeping and jeeps pulling rockets on wheels; later they passed a train of cars roped together with a cable, pulled by a closed-cab Massey Ferguson tractor. There were riders only in the back seats of the cars.

A few miles west of the river, the land began to flatten out. Plowed fields appeared. Now there were towns. Each was the same as the one before: a grain elevator, a crossing with one stoplight, a drugstore, a feed store, a few white houses and big trees. There was one town every ten or twelve miles, as regular as fence posts. The interstate never went through them, but around and slightly over on embankments which were the only curves and the highest points for miles in every direction. Otherwise, the world was as flat as a card table.

There were no tractors in the mile-long fields, no people on the block-long streets, no lights in the white houses under the elms. It was beginning to get dark.

The radio went off. Crystal sat up.

"Where are we?" she said, rubbing her eyes.

Just then a sign raced by, WELCOME TO OKLAHOMA.

They switched drivers without slowing down. Williams lifted off the seat, and she slid under him. They were getting good at it. He was worried about gas. The gauge still read a quarter tank, but he didn't trust it. He opened the glove compartment. The five .30-30 shells were rolling around loose. The map was wrapped around the little owl, which felt cold to touch, like it had been left in the freezer.

"We need gas pretty soon," Williams said. He spread the map across his knees. According to the map, the road they were on was the main four-lane heading across South Missouri and Oklahoma to the Mexico line. But it looked strange to Williams. Wasn't there another city besides Tulsa in Oklahoma? Wasn't there another state between Oklahoma and Mexico?

He couldn't be sure, and the longer he looked at the map, the righter it looked.

He went to sleep and dreamed about the half bridge high in the clouds. A fiddle player, balanced on the very end of it, was playing the "Orange Blossom Special." He was about to fall.

When a car's brakes lock, first it kneels, then it lifts and begins to glide gracefully like a skater in loops across the concrete, which magically becomes slick like maple furniture. At first the wailing of the tires has a wild and a mournful sound, like a fiddle . . .

Then it turns mean and sounds like screams.

The Chrysler was doing 88 when Crystal saw an open hole where the road should have been on an overpass over a county road. At first she thought it was a mirage, but she tapped the brakes just in case. Then she saw the concrete abutment on the other side of the hole. She stood on the brakes and the Chrysler, instead of stopping, went into a long, looping spin. Williams woke up and watched through the windshield as the sides of the road swapped places three times. Back east it was getting dark, to the west still red with sunset, to the north silvery with moonlight, and to the south there was what looked like a city across the turning plain.

Crystal was wondering what her mother was thinking when she died, when the car stopped, sideways, at the edge of the hole. Williams looked out his window and saw the county road twenty feet straight down. Lying on the road below were the yellow fifty-five-gallon drums that had been knocked down by the last car, which hadn't stopped in time. It lay upside down in a pool of shattered glass. As a transmission man, Williams could tell by the way the pipes fit around the tailhousing that it was a '72–'75 Buick.

"Shit," said Crystal.

On the horizon to the south, they saw tall signs for shopping centers. They were hungry. They were tired. They needed gas. When they moved to switch drivers, they noticed they were holding hands.

The county road turned into a four-lane. Heading south, they passed through subdivisions that looked like no one had moved in yet and stoplights that blinked on empty intersections. Then there were a few cars, more lights, some restaurants and shopping centers.

And finally a Mobil station.

The car had been driving with a slight thump, and while the attendant filled the tank, Williams checked the tires. Each one had a baseball-size flat spot from the long skid. Trying to look like he did it every day, he ordered a set of new radial tires, as well as a battery to sell.

The bill came to $284.69, and the attendant had to call it in before he could put the tires on. Meanwhile, Williams and Crystal were starving, without even fifty cents to buy a candy bar. The attendant, a skinny teenager in a Hedman Header hat, punched the card numbers into a grease-stained plastic keyboard.

The clicking sounded terrifyingly loud.

An asterisk appeared at the center of the screen, then words: THANK YOU FOR TRAVELING MOBIL

"Okay," the kid said. "Anything else?"

"Yeah," Crystal said. "Make that *two* sets of radials. Mount one set and put one set in the trunk for later."

The attendant looked at Williams, who tried to look made out of money, and shrugged. "It's your money."

He didn't call it in again.

Most of the stores in most of the shopping centers were closed, but there was a K-Mart and a McDonald's open in one. Teenagers sat on the hoods of their cars drinking beer in the parking lot. Williams sold the extra tires for a hundred dollars and threw in the battery.

"We're rich!" Crystal said, snapping the five twenties. "Let's stay at a motel."

Williams said, "Sure, why not?" He looked away, so she couldn't see he was blushing. Was it because of the holding hands? Hers had felt very small and warm in his.

First, they feasted at McDonald's, topping off fries and Big Macs with hot apple pie; then, they went shopping at K-Mart. The store was immense, brilliantly lighted, deserted. The only clerks were two elderly white women who stood by the cash registers eating popcorn from red-white-and-blue boxes. They seemed in a hurry to close. Williams bought a stiff new Levi jacket and an Oklahoma is OK sweatshirt. Crystal bought a shiny peach blouse and socks for him as well as her, then made him wait in the gun section while she picked out underwear. Williams wondered what she was buying. Was it for the motel? He encouraged his imagination to run wild.

Crystal had never stayed in a motel before, and she was looking forward to the experience.

They found a place called the Oh-Kay next door to a 7-Eleven. Crystal waited in the car while Williams registered them as Mr. and Mrs. Williams. The owner was an old woman who wanted the money in advance. It was $37.95, and Williams gave her the last two twenties and told her to keep the change.

"I will *not* keep the change," she said and counted out two ones and a nickel into his hand.

With Crystal on tiptoes looking over his shoulder, Williams unlocked the door and turned on the light.

It was everything she had expected. There were two blond wood beds, a huge color TV, and a dresser-desk combination with 12 drawers. Everything in the bathroom was ivory-colored, even the perfect tiny cake of soap. She opened the wrapper to take a peek, then wrapped it back up and replaced it in its dish. She sat on each bed and opened all twelve drawers. She flushed the almost noiseless toilet.

While Crystal took a shower, Williams went next door to the 7-Eleven and bought two Cokes and a box of vanilla wafers. Crystal was still in the shower when he got back. He wondered what she would be wearing when she came out. Should he get undressed? He decided not to. He brought the map and the owl in from the car, but he left the .30-30 shells in the glove compartment. He unfolded the map. If this was Tulsa, Ala Roja was about 300 miles away.

"One more day," he said through the door.

"What?"

The shower cut off. Williams backed away from the door. He could hear rustling. He sat down on the bed and popped open a Coke.

"I said we'll make it tomorrow," he said.

"Oh."

He saw the doorknob start turning. He turned out the overhead light. He checked the soles of his boots for holes.

She came out and crossed the room and turned on the overhead light and sat down on the bed beside him, still drying her hair. She was wearing long-sleeved blue flannel pajamas, decorated with pink panthers, with elastic at the wrists and ankles.

"Want some Coke?" he asked.

"No thanks." Excitedly, Crystal jumped up and sat on the other bed. She bounced up and down. She turned back the spread and slipped in between the sheets. She arranged the covers over herself exactly, smoothing them with her hands.

"I never stayed in a motel before," she said. "Isn't hit neat?"

Williams agreed that it was. He finished his Coke and took a cold shower. She had worn the soap down to a sliver. She was already asleep when he came out. He smoothed her covers, and she didn't stir. He smiled. He had to admit the joke was on him.

He folded the map and put it and the ice-cold owl into the drawer in the bedside table, then got under the covers in his own bed. He watched TV and ate the vanilla wafers and drank the other Coke himself.

After Williams was asleep, the TV came back on again. It was some kind of talk show. The woman with the white hair was the hostess, and two men were her guests. They were sitting on long couches. The man in the blue STP vest was holding a short shotgun across his lap, and it looked strange to see a gun on a talk show. The woman said something to him, then looked into the camera and laughed.

There was no sound, but the light from the TV changed colors.

First it was red and the drawer opened.

Then it was blue and the map unfolded.

It turned red again and the map folded back up.

It turned blue and the drawer closed.

Then the TV went off again.

16

NEITHER CRYSTAL NOR WILLIAMS had ever seen anything like the Great Plains before. Treeless and flat for hundreds of miles, they were more than just empty; they filled the heart of the continent like a sea.

The road ran straight as a string, south and west.

There was more traffic on the interstate than there had been the day before, all of it heading north and east on the other side of the median. There were military convoys. There were trucks filled with sheep and with cattle. There was another train of cars roped together, pulled by a tractor, filled with people looking thoughtfully out of the windows as if at a gloomier world than the one they'd expected.

It was the most spectacular country Williams had ever seen. It was the opposite of cluttered, wrinkled, green Kentucky. There were no trees, no hills, no rivers, no houses, no fences, no barns, just pure world untouched and unclaimed except for the streak of highway itself and, far above, the white streaks of jet vapor trails heading east and west.

It was late afternoon and the country was looking a little rougher when they got to Ala Roja. On the horizon there were flat-topped hills. The green-and-white metal sign at the edge of the highway was the first green thing in twenty miles.

Williams slowed and looked for an exit, but there was only the sign.

"Back up, that was hit," Crystal said.

"I can't just back up," Williams said. "I have to find a place to turn around."

"Sure you can. There hasn't been another car for a hundred miles."

The Chrysler topped a rise, and a few miles ahead they saw the Mexican border, the three-story-high fence lighted even in the day by the laser searchlights turning on the towers. At the gate there was a Stuckey's and an Exxon. At this distance, the crackling sound from the fence sounded like fireworks.

"If you don't want to back up, then turn around," Crystal said.

Williams stopped. Instead of crossing the dry, brown median, he punched the Chrysler into reverse and glided back smoothly at almost 50 for almost a half a mile, pulling up beside the sign.

ALA ROJA

It was standard highway white on green. There was no exit, but there was a break in the fence and two tracks in the red dirt leading up the side of a low mesa with a white rock rim. On the hillside there was a junkyard, with cars of all colors scattered among rose-colored rocks. Near the top, a white house trailer was set among the rocks. Wood smoke came from the trailer.

"That must be hit," Crystal said, wondering what to expect. Was this the end of her journey? Would Talking Man be here? She took the owl and the map out of the glove compartment and put them in her purse as Williams drove the Chrysler through the fence.

The hill was steeper than it looked.

The cars were well preserved—no rain, no rust, Williams figured—but the colors were all faded to the same dull tone by the sun.

The trailer was an old Kingsway American Eagle with a stovepipe sticking through the boarded-up picture window.

Hey Hoss's Dodge pickup was sitting in front—with the tires and windows all shot out. The radiator was still hissing steam.

"Wait!" Williams said, but Crystal had already jumped out of the car while it was still moving. She ran into the trailer. Williams put the Chrysler into park and followed. Across the plains to the north, he could see a rooster tail of dust heading toward the horizon.

The inside of the trailer was dark; the only light came from the doorway and a black-and-white TV that flickered in one corner. Crystal looked around the room for Talking Man, but he was nowhere to be seen. On the couch sat an old, old woman in a dirty white dress with her head in her hands, rocking back and forth. Her hair was black and gray. The front of her dress was covered with blood. Crystal lifted her chin and saw that she had been shot in the neck. The blood was pumping out in dark, regular streams.

Crystal backed away, but the woman opened one eye and took her hand and said something.

Hit's in Spanish, Crystal thought. She thinks I can understand.

The room got even darker, and she turned and saw Williams outlined in the doorway.

"Go get some help," she said.

"I don't want to leave you here alone."

"Get some alcohol and bandages at Stuckey's," Crystal said. "Hurry. She's been shot."

"But they might still be around."

"You saw their dust driving off," Crystal said. "Go on!"

Williams looked north. The rooster tail was longer and farther away. He left.

Crystal waited until she heard Williams drive off and then sat down beside the old woman on the couch. The old woman leaned her head back with a sigh. The blood was slowing down, and she didn't seem to be choking. She seemed worried, though. She kept one hand at her throat and pointed at the TV with the other.

"You want me to turn hit off?" Crystal asked.

The old woman shook her head and jabbed her finger at the TV. It was showing "I love Lucy" in Spanish. Crystal switched to the next channel, a game show.

The old woman shook her head.

Crystal switched again. A soap opera.

The old woman shook her head and jabbed her finger at the screen, hard, as if she wanted to punch through it.

Crystal reached behind the TV and found a jar. It

was the Mason jar Talking Man had gotten from the Ford in Owensboro. It was cold and heavy, and when she picked it up the thick clear liquid sloshed back and forth, rocking her whole body.

She handed it to the old woman, who held it in her blood-stained lap between her knees and gripped the top in both hands. Instead of unscrewing it, she screwed it on tighter, with a loud echoing sound.

Just then a car drove up.

That was quick, Crystal thought, thinking it was Williams. Then she heard two car doors slam.

Stuckey's was closed. It looked like it had been closed for a million years. The windows were boarded up, and when Williams peeked through he saw white places in the concrete where the fixtures had been ripped out. The cars he had seen from the interstate were just shells with no glass, no motors, no tires.

The crackling of the light fence was thunderous up close. The lasers swept across the desert from the towers, lighting the sixty-foot strip of border like sidewalk under a neon sign. Rabbits lay dead in the glare with their heads on backward.

The highway was blocked with a stack of burned cars. There was a guardhouse or tollbooth, but no one was in it.

Williams went across the road to the Exxon station. The cash register was wide open, and the pumps were knocked over. The phones were ripped out of the booths. The doors were torn off the rest rooms. He found a roll of toilet paper in the ladies' room and headed back, in the southbound lane, toward Ala Roja, holding the Chrysler wide open. He didn't like Crystal being there alone.

Barely slowing, he cut through the fence. The Chrysler was sprung stiff and high, never bottoming out even at 50 on the dirt. Starting up the rocky path between the cars, Williams sensed rather than heard the car coming down toward him; he pulled over just in time as it sped by, its frame striking sparks on the rocks.

It was the mystery car—the white car driven by the white-haired woman, the car he was sure had been wrecked back in South Missouri. The man in the STP vest sat beside her, holding something on his lap.

The cowboy sat in the backseat. Instead of a Buck knife, he was waving a pistol out the window. He looked even more like Hey Hoss than before.

He fired twice, and Williams ducked. Bullets whined off the rocks. Something hot flew past Williams's ear. The glass shattered on a '58 Ford by the road, and the white car was gone.

Then there was another, more ominous sound. The radio came on.

Williams spun back onto the road and roared up the hill.

Something had happened to Crystal!

Crystal ran for the screen door to lock it, but a boot kicked it open; the frame hit her face and she fell backward. She could taste blood on her lip.

A dark shape filled the doorway. Crystal crawled onto the couch beside the old woman, who sat unmoving, watching. She put her purse on the old woman's lap and took the Mason jar and tried to hide it.

The little cowboy with the rat moustache stepped through the door expertly opening a Buck knife with one hand.

Crystal stood up between him and the old woman.

The white-haired woman stood watching from the door, then slipped through.

Grinning, the cowboy put the knife to Crystal's throat and backed her up until she fell back onto the couch. He grabbed the jar; Crystal couldn't hold on.

The white-haired woman reached for the purse with the owl in it. The old woman pulled it back but lost it, pulled it back but lost it.

The white-haired woman ran out the door with the purse with the owl in it. The cowboy followed with the Mason jar. Then, at the door, he turned back and suddenly, laughing soundlessly as if at a joke, lunged at Crystal with the knife. She felt the 3½-inch blade slide into her chest, through her new peach blouse, right at the smooth top of her left breast.

She saw him grin, grin, grin.

She felt the cold point push in and push her heart to one side.

She felt herself fall over.

17

IT WAS TOO DARK to see inside the trailer, but Williams could hear snoring. He shut the screen door behind him and, by the TV light, saw Crystal and the old woman sitting side by side on the couch. They were both snoring. The old woman held an open Buck knife in her lap. Crystal's new peach blouse was wadded up in her lap, and she was wearing only her jeans and a bra. Her new bra was pink on one side and dark red on the other, which looked odd, like a clown bra, until Williams saw it was blood. At the top of her left breast there was a half-moon-shaped white scar.

He looked at her throat and her back. She was snoring softly. He couldn't find any other wounds on her.

The old woman's throat had stopped bleeding. Now

blood was soaking through the front of her white dress from her heart. She quit snoring and opened one eye and reached out her hand. Williams gave her the wad of toilet paper from the Exxon station, which she held against her breast.

She seemed to be struggling to say something.

"Coche," she whispered finally.

The car.

Williams ran outside. The Chrysler was still idling where he had parked it behind Hey Hoss's shot-up truck. But something was wrong. A dark stain was spreading under the car onto the sand. He looked underneath. Red transmission fluid was pumping out of a bullet hole in the transmission case. The stream slowed even as he watched.

He shut the engine off.

In the distance under the white full moon, another rooster tail of dust was heading north, following the first one.

To the east, the sky was darkening as the long day drew toward its end.

"Williams?"

From the exact center of this world of sky and plain and rim, from inside the trailer, Crystal was calling him.

There was a hand pump at the kitchen end of the trailer. Williams pumped, his eyes turned away, while Crystal washed the old woman's face and hands and helped her off with her dress. She was no longer bleeding, but her wrinkled old body was covered with scars. Crystal wrapped her in another old white cotton dress, exactly like the one she had taken off, from a trunk of them, all the same. Then she made Williams close his eyes and pump while she took off her bra and washed herself.

She touched the little scar at the top of her breast and shivered. She could remember the cold blade pushing in. She could remember the old woman pulling it out.

The left cup of her bra was stiff with blood, and it wouldn't wash out. She wished now that she'd bought two bras at K-Mart or hadn't left her old one in the motel wastebasket. Her new peach blouse was ruined with blood, and there was a neat little slit over the left pocket.

She dropped it and the bra into the trash and put on Williams's Oklahoma is OK sweatshirt from the car before he was allowed to open his eyes again.

"She wants us to carry her outside," Crystal said.

The old woman was sitting up on the couch, smoothing her white dress across her knees. She had big turquoise rings on her fingers, and one finger on her left hand was missing.

"How do you know what she wants anyway?"

"Hit's like Talking Man," Crystal said. "She doesn't exactly talk to me, but I can understand what she's saying. I can hear her in the back of my eyes." She took one of the old woman's arms, and Williams got the other.

There was an aluminum lawn chair covered with a Mexican blanket by the front door of the trailer. They sat the old woman in it, overlooking a hundred miles of desert to the swiftly darkening north and east. To the west, the sky was red like soup.

"Since when do you speak Spanish?" Williams said.

"How do you know she speaks Spanish if you can't hear her? And why are you so mad anyway?"

He was mad because the car was ruined.

"She says she wants to help you fix the car."

"Not fixable," Williams said. "There's a hole shot in the transmission."

Crystal arranged layers of shawls over the old woman's shoulders. "She says look in the trailer behind the TV, propped in the corner."

Williams went in and came out with an ancient Winchester lever action, a "yellowboy" .30-30 even older than the Model 94. He had seen it in magazines but had never held one before. This one was in poor condition. Thumbtacks had been pressed into the stock in a crude imitation of silver studs. He jacked the lever open; the chamber was empty.

The old woman pointed to the Chrysler. Williams remembered the five shells and got them out of the glove compartment. They fit.

"What does she want me to do, put it out of its misery?"

Crystal was kneeling in the sand, arranging sticks to build a fire.

"This old gun's as loose as a widow's barn," Williams said, shaking it to show Crystal. "If I'm lucky, it won't even fire. If it does, it'll probably blow up."

Crystal ignored his sarcasm, intent on building her fire. First she laid an egg carton pointing north and south. Then she piled little sticks against it, like a lean-to built onto a trailer. Then she stood up, dusting off her knees.

"She says go down through the junkyard," Crystal said, "around the bluff to the west, till you come to a light brown '54 Buick hardtop. She says there you are to wait."

"There he is to wait," Williams said. "You're even starting to talk like her."

But he went.

The old woman watched while Crystal heated up some canned tomato soup on the little stick fire, but when Crystal tried to feed her some, she shook her head. All she would take was whiskey, with water, in a paper cup. There was a fifth in the refrigerator in the trailer, which is where Talking Man used to keep whiskey; and not just any whiskey, but Kentucky Tavern, Talking Man's favorite brand. Crystal thought this was a good sign.

But where was Talking Man? Why had he come here? Had he gotten away?

Crystal spooned the soup straight out of the saucepan and ate it with white bread. She was hungry, but she saved some for Williams.

The whiskey seemed to wake the old woman up. She started mumbling, and Crystal tried to listen, but she only occasionally understood. Like Williams looking for Talking Man, she could understand better if she didn't listen hard.

To the south, the border looked like an amusement park, with funny noises and lights flashing. Every ten minutes there was a thumping noise as the robot 'copter flew the line.

To the north, the moon got bright as the sky got darker. It was bigger than ever. The clouds were steam, the old woman told her, from cracks that were opening in the surface. The fires were forests of oxygen crystals burning.

Crystal kept the fire small and the woodpile big. Now that the twigs were gone, she burned boards, old and silvery like driftwood from the sky.

She heard a shot, and she pushed the soup close to the fire to warm up. Williams would be heading back now.

The cars were scattered around the curve of the bluff under the rock rim like charms on a necklace. It was different from a junkyard in Kentucky. There were no weeds, no little trees growing through hoods or out of empty trunks, no lake-size puddles between the cars, no rich thick mud. The cars were bleached by the sun but not rusted, and all were old: the newest were from the seventies, and most were from the fifties and sixties.

Williams wondered how he was supposed to find a transmission for the Chrysler, and even if he did, what was he supposed to do, shoot it out?

On the west side of the bluff, he found the brown '54 Buick. It was a Century four-door sedan, not a hardtop, with no tires, no hood, and no manifold or heads on the block; but the doors and the windshield were intact.

It was dark everywhere but in the west, where the clouds on the horizon still glowed hot red. To the north, the moon was smoky with its centuries-old fires.

The inside of the Buick was clean, and Williams got into the driver's seat. Through the windshield, he watched the clouds go out like coals.

He must have fallen asleep and dreamed he was driving, because he woke up panicked. There were no lights. He saw a thousand miles of darkness over the steering wheel. Then he remembered where he was.

Something was banging on the roof. He opened the door and looked up, and something white jumped over his head.

It hit the dirt and leaped again, to the top of the next car, a '64 Chevy Nova, and stopped, looking back at him curiously.

It was an antelope.

Even though he had never seen one before, it looked familiar. It was a small creature combining the helpless beauty of a deer and the foolish dignity of a goat.

He looked at it, and it looked at him.

He flapped his arms to see what it would do. It jumped back one step but didn't run.

He held out a hand but it didn't move forward.

It had an expectant look in its eye. While it watched, he slowly slid the gun across the seat into his hands. He knew what he was supposed to do even though he didn't particularly want to do it.

18

WILLIAMS CAME BACK WITH the antelope over his shoulder. The old woman looked pleased. With gestures and pointing she directed Williams while he tied the antelope's heels together and hung it from a hook on the side of the trailer. The ground under the hook was dark. Williams wiped off the Buck knife and drew a line with his finger across the antelope's throat.

The old woman shook her head. One more thing.

She sent Crystal back into the trailer for a dishpan, which she carefully wiped on her dress; then Crystal placed it under the antelope's head.

Now the old woman nodded. Williams cut the antelope's throat.

Blood filled the dishpan with a sound of bells.

The old woman drew a line down her own belly; Williams slit the animal's belly open.

The old woman pointed to Crystal, and Crystal reached into the antelope's belly. It wasn't warm but cold. She felt something strange and pulled it out. It was an owl in a plastic sandwich bag.

How's this going to fix my car? Williams wondered. But he was feeling better. It was magic, and he knew it worked at least some of the time.

According to Talking Man, Crystal said, there were only three things wrong with Kentucky Tavern whiskey: It was a little too old, a little too rich, and a little too fine for everyday consumption. They all had a drink.

The fire was crackling; the moon was up, huger than ever before. The old woman sat and watched from the aluminum chair, and Crystal tended the fire, while Williams put the blood in the transmission. Under the trailer he found a goose-necked funnel and three cans of K-Mart transmission fluid. You always add fluid to a transmission while it's running, so he started the Chrysler and alternated a quart of fluid and a quart of blood, as the old woman suggested.

"You're making hit worse," Crystal said, kneeling to look under the car. "Hit's leaking again."

"It only quit because it was empty," Williams said. He poured in one more can of each.

"Hit's slowing down a little."

One more can of blood and one more can of transmission fluid made six, the capacity of the Torqueflite transmission.

"Hit's just dripping now."

Williams was grinning. He let it drip for a while and

then topped it off with the last of the antelope blood, a half a can. He let it idle for another five minutes while he ate some soup, then checked it again. It was still full. It seemed to have stopped dripping. Drive and reverse both caught okay. He shut the engine off.

Crystal was sitting next to the old woman's chair on a five-gallon paint can, smoking a cigarette and staring at the fire.

"Tell her we appreciate the magic trick," Williams said happily. He stretched out on the ground with his head on a log.

"She says Talking Man has gone to the North Pole," Crystal said. "She says we have to go after him." She looked over to see Williams's reaction to this news. He was already asleep.

The old woman held Crystal's hand and talked, and the night got deeper. The moon was as steady as a continent in the north. Williams slept with the rifle beside him. Crystal felt tears stream down her face although she wasn't crying; she felt as if the old woman's sorrow was passing in through her hand and out through her eyes into the night.

She was talking in Spanish, and Crystal could understand bits and pieces of it if she kept herself from listening and let it run by.

"She says there is a city at the top of the world," Crystal said, even though Williams was sleeping. It helped her understand, to say it out loud. "Edminidine."

"Dice que esta una ciudad al punto del mundo."

Though Crystal didn't realize it, the old woman was slipping backward from Spanish to Latin, and even deeper, into forgotten tongues older than the rings on her fingers. Crystal slipped with her.

There is a passage between the end of time and its beginning, between Edminidine and Elennor—a well with sky at both ends. There she has gone with the unbeen.

Who is she?

She is his lover, Dgene.

Lover? What about my mother?

Before and after your mother, there is Dgene.

Who are you?

Before and after you, there is me.

There is a city at the top of the world.

"Edminidine."

There is a tower at the end of time.

"Elennor."

Williams stirred but didn't wake up.

Crystal covered him with a blanket from the trailer and stirred the fire.

Talking Man has gone there.

Elennor.

Edminidine.

They are connected.

The well.

The tower.

A well is a tower into the world.

Talking Man must take the owl and stop her before she lets the unbeen through.

The unbeen.

It is small enough to fit in a jar and big enough to cover the world.

That. Crystal shivered.

You have seen it. You have held it in your hand.

It is cold.

He must take the owl and stop her before she lets the unbeen through.

Or the world will end.

Worse than that. Listen, child.

She listened.

But Talking Man doesn't have the owl. They took it.

You do.

It is the same?

It is.

What about my tobacco?

It waits for you.

Will Talking Man come home?

Talking Man will go home.

Who are you?

She told her.

The fire was blazing. Crystal sat up. Had she been asleep too? The fire was bright yet cold, and as she watched, it went out like a gas flame, the blue ball rising slightly into the air and disappearing suddenly.

The old woman was dead. Her hand in Crystal's was cold, cold, cold.

Crystal didn't feel sad anymore. She took the blanket from Williams and covered the old woman's body. She found a cigarette butt in the ashtray of the Chrysler and waited for dawn, too wired up to sleep. She had a drink of whiskey. She couldn't remember most of what they had talked about. She missed Talking Man. She was glad Dgene hadn't killed him.

Dawn came and they headed out.

19

CRYSTAL DROVE DUE WEST across the plain instead of following the dirt track north. She couldn't tell where she had gotten the idea but it was deep, like a memory, and unexplorable, like a dream. Maybe the old woman had left it there. At dawn, Crystal and Williams had wrapped her in a blanket and stretched her out on the couch in the trailer. Crystal had scratched out the fire and scattered the ashes, turned off the TV and closed the old woman's eyes; then she pulled the trailer door shut. It wasn't quite daylight. Williams levered the four shells out of the Winchester and threw it into the back seat. He was still tired, but he couldn't go back to sleep until he heard how the transmission sounded.

Crystal followed a track around the base of the hill, then struck out straight across the trackless, brushless, desertlike plain, due west, toward low distant clouds. The Chrysler upshifted smoothly with no slipping or funny smells. By the time it was in high, Williams was asleep with his head on Crystal's lap.

Crystal had been up all night, but she wasn't tired. Her head was still filled with the old woman's talk. She could still feel her hand growing colder. She found the last Marlboro in the last pack from the K-Mart carton and cruised on at almost 40 on the dirt, the Chrysler outrunning its dust like a jet outruns its sound.

After thirty miles of dirt, she hit a north-south interstate and got on through a gap in the fence. She headed north, toward the huge moon that never rose and never set. Williams woke up, and they switched drivers without slowing down. They had gone as far west as they could go. Running parallel to the highway to the left was a wall of stone and snow higher than anything Crystal had ever seen or even imagined before, though Williams knew it well from books: the Rockies.

As always, there was the problem of gasoline. By noon Williams had driven a hundred miles and seen only one station, the wrong kind, a Major. He had never even heard of it. He hoped the world wasn't changing so much that there were no more Mobil stations; if it did, they were in trouble. Unless the card changed too.

He checked it. It was still Mobil.

It felt good to let the 413 stretch out a little. 80, 90, was its natural speed. The gas gauge hovered at a quarter. This interstate wasn't in as good shape as the last one; there were big breaks in the pavement, and sometimes it narrowed to just one lane around some wrecked cars. Once, it was almost blocked by a wrecked chicken truck covered with black buzzards like giant flies; they didn't scatter but just turned their heads to watch as the Chrysler edged past.

But no bridges were down, and in the daylight it seemed safe to let the Chrysler run on out.

Crystal slept like a baby, curled up with her cheek against the back of her hand and her head against the door. That meant Williams could listen to the radio. There were only two stations, one country and one Spanish, both very faint; but gradually, as they went north, the country station came in better and better.

Williams finally saw a Mobil sign in the distance—one of those signs on poles that are taller than a tree and not as big as a hill, an in-between size unique in nature.

The radio went off and on again as he slowed down, as if it had a bad connection; Crystal stretched and went back to sleep.

The station was run by a teenager in a Champion Spark Plug hat. The transmission oil looked fine and didn't even smell strange; nobody would guess it was fifty percent blood. Williams filled the car with gas and bought a battery, which he sold back to the kid for twelve dollars. From machines he bought candy bars, cold drinks, cheese crackers and Marlboros.

"So what happened to Talking Man?" Williams asked the next time the radio went off.

"He got away," Crystal said, snuggling against his shoulder but not opening her eyes. "They tried to kill him, but she saved him and he got away."

"She. Who is she, anyway?"

"You won't believe me if I tell you."

"Try me."

"She says she's . . . my daughter." Crystal opened one eye.

"You're right. I don't believe you."

"See."

"You don't have a daughter."

"She says I will."

"Tell me this: How come Hey Hoss shot up his own truck?"

"He's not exactly Hey Hoss. He sort of is. She can imitate people. Make them do crazy things."

"Like shoot up their own trucks."

"Uh huh."

"So where are we headed now?"

"The North Pole."

The radio came on again.

The moon never rose and never set. It hung in the north, appearing and disappearing behind dark clouds that covered it like smoke. Conway Twitty was singing when suddenly the radio went off.

"I was having a bad dream," Crystal said. She checked the glove compartment. The owl in the sandwich bag was still there. "Where are we?"

"Coming to Denver," Williams said. Crystal sat up and looked around. To the east, the plains were like a sea, stretching treeless as far as the eye could see and a thousand miles beyond that. To the west, the mountains rose like a cliff made out of whole counties. The lower slopes were barren, like the plains; there was a tree line where the trees began, then another where they ended, giving way to grass again; then red and gray stone; then, at the top, gold and silver streaked with snow, like bad places the moon had scraped.

To the north, Denver was burning.

20

WILLIAMS HAD WATCHED THE smoke of the city for miles before realizing what it was. It was late and the sky was already darkening to the east; the moon was hidden behind the black mushrooming tower of what he had thought for forty miles was rain clouds, stretching all the way to the top of the sky. They switched drivers without slowing down, both watching it, fascinated; it was beautiful in a grim way. The rolling ledges high up were lighted orange from the bottom and glowed, even though they could see no flames anywhere.

"Wonder what happened."

"You got me."

The Chrysler sped toward it fearlessly.

*   *   *

There was no traffic, but Crystal slowed gradually as the interstate became littered with glass and the shells of cars. They were inside the outskirts of Denver, according to the signs. The road got rougher, and finally it was blocked by a two-car-high wall of wrecks turned on their sides, just past an exit. Crystal pulled off, squeezing between the orange drums, down onto a two-lane that led into a four-lane that led north, then east.

Down here, the wind was carrying paper and trash, leaves and even shingles in a rolling storm toward the black column that filled the sky ahead and overhead. There was no smell of smoke, since the wind was all heading into the fire.

Now they saw other cars, mostly heading east on the four-lane between empty shopping plazas. Crystal cut north on another four-lane that seemed as if it might skirt the burning city. But it turned into a two-lane, and the traffic slowed, then jammed to a stop in a residential neighborhood with all the side roads blocked. Soldiers in orange and gray sat on the unmowed lawns, smoking with their cigarettes cupped in their hands, under trees as naked as February trees, stripped by the firestorm wind.

There was a roadblock ahead.

Two tanks were wedged across the road, their tracks sinking into the asphalt and their guns pointing straight into the blocks-long line of traffic. The cars crept forward slowly while boys in Ortega Chili hats walked up and down the line selling tortillas wrapped around cold, unidentifiable meat.

"How much?" Williams asked.

"Two dollars."

It was all he had left, but he bought one and they shared it, both sick of candy bars.

The cars in the line were mostly old junkers with Colorado or San Luis plates, packed with families and all their possessions: pets, children, mattresses, TVs, pots and pans. Most of the people looked Mexican. The line crept slowly forward until Crystal and Williams were twelfth back from the roadblock, then tenth. Now they could see what was happening. At the roadblock, a Mexican family was made to get out of their '75 Chevy and stand spread-eagled, even the kids, while they were searched; their stuff was piled on the sidewalk, and a soldier drove the car through the roadblock with the trunk still open. The people were led into one of the houses. A woman in a white dress opened the door for them. One of the kids didn't want to go and she picked him up. She was wearing rubber gloves.

The next car was driven by a woman alone, but the routine was the same.

Williams got out of the car to pee in the shrubbery of a house. From the yard, he could see the roadblock more clearly. One of the men checking off cars on a clipboard looked familiar.

"Turn around," Williams whispered, getting back into the car.

"What?"

"Turn around," Williams said, whispering. "I saw Hey Hoss."

Crystal strained to see through the darkness. She saw the soldiers by the tank; either cigarettes were scarce or they were passing a joint. Was it her imagination? They all looked a little like Hey Hoss to her.

"Under the trees," Williams said.

Crystal saw two men under a bare cottonwood in the yard checking off cars on a clipboard: One was an officer in a silver plastic helmet, and the other was a civilian in sunglasses. The civilian lifted his glasses. He looked more like Hey Hoss than the others.

"Is hit the real guy?" Crystal asked.

"Let's don't wait around to find out."

Crystal found reverse and eased the long tail of the Chrysler up over the curb, into the yard behind her; she cut the wheel and punched the Chrysler into drive. She pulled out slowly into the empty southbound lane . . . then hit it.

Hard.

Looking back, Williams saw soldiers running across the lawns, but he couldn't find Hey Hoss.

Tires screaming, the Chrysler was up to 60 in 9.7 seconds, running lightless down the wide, dark, hopefully empty street.

70.

Williams listened for shots or the sound of a siren. There was nothing. Then there was something worse: the whump whump whump of a helicopter.

"Turn off the lights!" Williams said. Crystal looked at him like he was stupid and smacked the knob to show him they had never been turned on. The light in front of the car was coming from overhead.

Williams leaned out the window. A searchlight was overhead, boring down closer and closer. He loaded the rifle and thought about taking a shot at the light—then he thought of the weapons they probably had up there. He pulled his head back in.

The whump whump grew louder. The light grew brighter. An electric voice barked: "PULL OVER."

Ahead was the interstate, shooting over the streets at rooftop level, north, into the black cloud of smoke. The entrance was blocked with yellow drums. The underpass was blocked with crossed striped poles.

They were trapped.

The pool of searchlight went from white to blue to white to blue again. "PULL OVER," barked the voice.

Instead, Crystal threw the Chrysler into a long slide up the entrance ramp, squeezing between the yellow drums; Williams winced as they rolled off the front fenders, ringing like deep bells.

Crystal turned on the headlights; a quarter of a mile ahead was a rolling, boiling wall of thick black smoke. There was a burst of automatic fire behind and the whump whump whump getting closer.

"Are you going to do what I think you're going to do?" Williams said.

She was.

Straight into the rolling wall of smoke they plunged.

21

THE WHOLE WORLD WAS smoke. With the lights on dim, so that they reflected less, Crystal could see only ten feet past the hood. She slowed to 30, then 25, following the white line. It was like driving into a cloud. There was no thump thump thump, no voices, no shots. She slowed to 20. The temptation was to stop altogether. But what then? She eased the Chrysler back up to 25 and held it steady, stitching the white line into the seam between her left front fender and hood.

Williams checked the vents and checked the windows, rolling them up as tightly as possible, then sat with his palms pressed together between his knees. It was hard, not driving; nothing to do but worry.

Whatever had set the city on fire could also have broken the bridges and overpasses, like the one that had almost gotten them in Oklahoma.

Crystal had been driving then, too.

But if they stopped or even slowed down they would die from the smoke.

They might die from it anyway.

What if they ran into the fire.

What if the smoke went on for a hundred miles. Or even ten.

What happened when the air inside the car gave out. The smoke was already beginning to leak in around the windows.

Or was it.

Even if it wasn't sooner or later it would.

And what was the car running on. Could a carburetor breathe smoke any better than a person.

What happened when the engine coughed and stopped.

"Light me a cigarette," Crystal said.

"Are you crazy?"

"No."

"Here we are about to suffocate and die of smoke, and you want to smoke."

"We're either going to make hit or not," she said. "I'm as scared as you are. Either way, I need a cigarette."

"No way," Williams said. "Just keep driving and forget it."

At least the thump thump thump was gone. There were no sounds at all. If they were driving through a fire, Williams couldn't see it anywhere—no lights or flames or shapes of buildings on either side. There was nothing but the blunt cave the headlights made in the rock-colored smoke.

What was the engine running on? The 413 never missed a lick. 35. 35. 35.

"Look out!"

By the time Williams saw it, Crystal had already missed it by less than a foot: a burned-out hulk of a car upside down in the left lane. It was impossible to tell if it was still smoking or not, since the air itself was smoke. If it had been sideways, they would have hit it. Crystal slowed to 30. There was another wreck, this one definitely burning with little orange flames climbing on the seat backs. She slowed to 25.

"Maybe we're getting toward the center," she said.

What if the road is blocked, Williams thought.

There was a wreck to the right and a wreck to the left, and Crystal snaked between them at 15 miles per hour. Williams tried to imagine what it would be like to sit and wait for the car to fill with smoke, or to get out and walk. Then he tried not to.

"Are you crying?" he asked.

She shook her head, wiping her eyes with the back of her hand. It was definitely getting smoky inside the car. She speeded back up to 25. Glass and trash crackled under the tires. Now there were orange flames through the smoke on both sides.

It was hazy inside the car but Williams couldn't smell smoke. Or maybe he was just used to it. It wasn't hard to breathe. Or was it. The dashboard and dial console of the Chrysler was glowing like a little city seen through the mist. It was as beautiful as a song.

Song.

The radio had come on.

Crystal was slumped down with her head leaning

against the wheel and they were heading into the rear of an overturned GMC van.

Williams took the wheel and the tires screamed as he found the white line again. Close. They were so good at switching drivers that they could do it even with Crystal asleep; she raised up and he slid under her, then she settled back down on his lap. He was getting sleepy too. Ahead, something was different; the line was too bright . . .

They were through.

He rolled down the windows and the car filled with air like cold water.

An endless sea of dark suburban roofs stretched northward under the beautiful, bright, too big, belted with moon clouds, moon.

22

THEY SLEPT PARKED UNDER an overpass out of sight of helicopters.

When Williams woke up it was daylight, but just barely: a gray daylight scratchy with dust and wind. Crystal was stretched out on the seat with her head on his shoulder. The car was rocking gently in the wind. The radio was on but it was just static. He turned it off.

He got out of the car to pee. Even though the air was filled with paper, trash and dust, it felt clean and unused, pouring down from the north.

Behind, to the south, the black fire-cloud rolled upward then spread out to become the black sky itself.

Far to the north, the sky was blue.

All around were redwood and *Compotex* row houses with infant stripped trees in the yards. Most of the houses seemed empty, but Williams saw what might have been a child's face in one window. From a driveway down the street he could hear a car trying to start, trying to start, trying to start.

When he got back into the Chrysler, Crystal was awake.

In a small shopping center they found a donut store with the plate-glass window broken, and they stepped through. The coffee in the pots was cold. The cash register was gone. The cigarette machine had been opened and emptied.

Crystal filled a white paper bag with powdered sugar donuts so stale they rattled.

"Hurry up," Williams said. "This is looting. We could get shot."

Nobody shot them. They entered the interstate at an exit by pushing two orange barrels aside, and headed north. Soon the smoke of Denver was far behind. The moon was huge but dim, unmoving above the northern horizon.

Williams drove. Crystal filled up on donuts and curled up against the door.

Snow-streaked mountains marched north alongside the highway to the west. To the east, the plains rolled off as featureless and grand as a sea. 80, 85. The radio came on. The gas stayed on a quarter.

They passed three gas stations, twenty miles apart— Shell, Viva, and Exxon—before Williams saw a Mobil sign. It looked odd, and yet it looked right. As he pulled in he checked the card in his wallet. Mobil, of course. Why did he have the feeling it had changed? How would he know if it had?

Crystal woke up as Williams pulled up to the pump.

The station was boarded up with three-by-nine plywood sheets, and one of the sheets scraped sideways, opening like a sliding door. A man in an I'm Saved Are You? hat stepped through. Behind him, a teenage girl held a single-shot 12-gauge with a cheap yellow wood stock.

A sign scrawled in red paint on the plywood said: GAS ONLY, NO OIL, CREDIT CARDS

"Does that mean you do take credit cards," Williams asked, "or does it mean you don't?"

"Means what it says," the man said. "Means we don't take cash."

"Fill her up with high-test."

The man crooked his finger over his shoulder, and the girl turned on a switch hidden in the darkness. The man pumped the gas.

"Nice day," Williams said.

The man nodded. "It's always a nice day in heaven." He reached for the Mobil card, but Williams pulled it back.

"Bring the little thing out here."

The man crooked his finger at the girl, and she brought the bill stamper out. He held the gun while she ran the card through, then gave it back to Williams.

"You all got any Cokes?" Crystal asked.

The man shook his head.

"Cigarettes?"

The man shook his head.

"Well, so long," Williams said.

"Hit's been real nice talking to you," Crystal said.

Heading north, they saw pirates. Crystal drove and they passed slow cars filled with families, with mattresses, sofas, TVs and stereos tied on top. The kids always waved but the grown-ups never did. There was more traffic, but the cars were strung out with lots of distance between them, and when the Chrysler passed they would pull over to give them plenty of room.

Crystal and Williams soon found out why.

They were going 75 when a black Peugeot passed them and disappeared into the flat, hazy distance. A few miles up the road they caught up with it again. It had forced an '82 Olds diesel station wagon onto the shoulder. A man stood with his head and shoulders sticking out of the Peugeot's sunroof, holding an Uzi. One of the windows of the station wagon was gone and kids inside were screaming.

Williams got the Winchester from the back seat and held it across his lap as they drove on north. It was still loaded from the night before.

The Peugeot passed them again an hour later, speeding toward its next victim.

North, north, north.

Williams drove while Crystal slept.

It got dark.

At a big interchange there was a gas station where Williams filled the car again. The gauge wouldn't move from a quarter. He bought a battery and resold it for twenty-five dollars and he and Crystal each had a hamburger and french fries, a Coke and apple pie, and potato chips to go. It was the first restaurant since Oklahoma. Most of the traffic went east and they headed north alone, the road like a seam between the mountains and the plains.

* * *

CONSTRUCTION
DANGER
RIGHT LANE ENDS

Crystal slowed down. She hadn't been asleep, but she had been driving in a kind of a daze. The country had changed. The mountains to the west were gone and so were the plains to the east. The highway was winding through pine-covered hills.

CAUTION
CONSTRUCTION
LEFT LANE ENDS

The road ended in a line of orange drums, with an arrow pointing to an exit. Crystal drove down into the forest, which was not as dark as it looked. The moonlight shone through the pines as if they were glass; the smooth floor of the forest gleamed.

The exit led onto a wide, straight gravel road, still heading north. Crystal eased the Chrysler back up to 55, then suddenly slammed on the brakes when a green Ford pickup pulled out in front of her and stopped in the center of the road.

The Chrysler slid to a stop. The back of the truck was filled with armed men.

Williams had been sleeping but now he was awake.

"Pirates," Crystal said.

Williams reached down to the floor for the rifle, but Crystal stopped his hand. A woman carrying a rifle was walking toward the car, with two men following behind her.

She was Black, about thirty, with short hair and a New York Yankees hat. She was wearing fatigues and carrying an M16. One of the men was carrying a Kalashnikov, and the other held a flashlight in Crystal's eyes.

"Just be cool," the woman said. "Just get out and open the trunk, please."

Crystal got out and opened the trunk. It was empty except for the spare.

"Just checking," the woman said. "You can get back in the car."

Crystal got back in the car.

"Where you all going?" the woman asked.

"North," Williams said.

"Canada," Crystal said.

"No way," the woman said. "We'll let you go back the way you came. We'll even let you keep the cowboy momento"—she pointed at the Winchester Williams was trying to cover with his legs—"but you can't go north. They've closed the border tighter than a preacher's asshole."

"Who?" Williams asked.

"Who do you think? The Bible clubs. One other thing. Got any cigarettes?"

Crystal checked the rearview mirror when she got back onto the interstate. No one was following. She cut off her headlights and headed down the first exit to the west.

"Why don't we head back?" Williams said. "She said we can't get through."

"Head back where? To Denver?"

Williams was quiet. She was right. Where was there to go back to?

Crystal turned north on a gravel road like the one where they had been stopped. After a few miles, it turned into a bulldozed swath through the trees. They switched drivers and Williams followed it north for an hour at a walking pace, the car rocking like a ship in rough water. Then the bulldozed area ended, and there was only a logging road leading between the trees up a steep hill.

It was even slower going because of the stumps. Williams winced every time he heard the oil pan, or worse, the patched transmission, scrape.

The road got steeper. The trees got bigger. The air got cooler. According to the moon, they were no longer headed just north, but west as well. Then the road ended at a cleared strip, twice as wide as a small river, that was cut straight east and west through the trees.

The border.

Crystal was asleep with her head against the door. Williams decided to wait until morning to cross. There was a funny sweet smell. There might be gas or lasers or a wire fence he couldn't see in the moonlight. He put his head on Crystal's lap, turned the radio off, and went to sleep.

He heard big animals crashing around in the forest, or was it a dream?

23

CRYSTAL AND WILLIAMS BOTH dreamed they dreamed the same dream: of a sea of dark shapes rocking the car, a sea of dark shapes rocking the car. But it was no dream. They woke up suddenly and lay silently holding each other while great shoulders rubbed against the car. A tramping noise filled the air. Antlers clicked together and knocked against the glass. A stream of caribou was splitting around the Chrysler like brown water around a red and white rock, running in a heavy million-hearted whisper north across the forest floor. It seemed like hours and then they were gone, all at once. Williams and Crystal watched through the windshield as the caribou streamed across the moon-washed border strip and into the dark Canadian forest. Then they went back to sleep.

Williams was awakened by an explosion.

He heard barking.

It was daylight. The caribou were gone. He saw a moose in the center of the border strip, surrounded by a pack of white wolves. The moose lay in a small crater that was muddy with blood; two of his legs had been blown off and were lying a few feet away. The wolves sat patiently on their haunches, as still and white as leftover snowdrifts, waiting for the moose to die. His antlers were heavy and his chin was hairy; he looked old.

The white wolves were silent. The barking came from the trees a few yards down the hill from the car, where gray wolves paced restlessly at the American edge of the strip.

The moose raised his face to the moon and groaned, yellow teeth gleaming. The gray wolves on the American side went crazy. One of them leaped into the cleared strip and ran toward the dying moose—then the ground lifted the wolf up, and there was a blast, and he fell dead.

The white wolves watched silently.

Crystal sat up rubbing her eyes.

The moose was dead. The white wolves, nine of them, moved smoothly in. The gray wolves howled jealously. Another one broke from the trees and ran for the moose, making it almost all the way before the ground ripped open and sent him flying. Two hideous sounds, a blast and a wet thump, came almost together.

"The strip is mined," Williams said.

"Look, they're wearing necklaces," Crystal said. She pointed at the white wolves. They were all wearing silver necklaces.

*   *   *

Williams stood at the edge of the trees. Crystal sat on the hood of the car. They could see now what was going on. The border had been seeded with antipersonnel mines that were set off by any animal that wasn't wearing a protective necklace. The caribou must have had them. The white wolves, formerly an endangered species, had them and now they ruled the strip, where they fed on the border kill.

Other animals, like the gray wolves, fed on their leavings.

The forest floor was littered with bones. They crackled under Williams's feet like leaves as he walked toward the car. He remembered the sweet smell from last night. It hadn't gone away; he had just gotten used to it. It was death. Death was all around. What he had at first thought were squirrels, were rats, scurrying across the forest floor. To the west, a small herd of caribou stepped into the border strip, testing the wind with big velvety noses.

Williams sat down beside Crystal on the hood of the car. They shared the last of the potato chips and stared across the border at the huge dim moon. There was an electric buzzing sound. It was flies: flies in clouds around the craters in the strip; flies in clouds around the shreds of meat that had blown into the trees. They were in the land of flies.

"There must be a way across," Crystal said.

"Are you crazy? We have to go back."

"Go back where?"

There was that question again.

Williams was gone almost an hour.

Crystal heard the crack of the old .30-30. Williams

came back running, carrying only the rifle, out of breath. He had killed a caribou but he couldn't cut the necklace off. They had to hurry before the wolves got it.

Crystal started the car while Williams jumped in; then she backed down the hill, winding through the wide spaces between the trees.

The gray wolves were already snapping at the caribou. Williams had only three shells left, so he chased them away, swinging the rifle like a club.

Crystal knelt down over the beast and closed its big reindeer eyes. Even though neither of them had ever seen one before, it was as familiar as Christmas. The wolves had only gnawed one hindquarter, and in the front the caribou looked almost unhurt, with just a tiny hole in its breast where it had been heart-shot.

The necklace was a silver cable with a small green microchip encased in epoxy. Williams tried to cut the cable, but it just dulled the Buck knife. Neither of them wanted to saw off the caribou's head, so they pulled the whole animal up onto the hood. Williams leaned out the window and held one leg, so it wouldn't slide off, while Crystal drove slowly back through the trees to where the road ended.

Crystal pulled the last cigarette out of her last pack, straightened it and lit it. Then she nosed the Chrysler out of the trees, onto the cleared ground. Williams held his knees together. Crystal squeezed one eye shut and then the other. There was no explosion. She drove across the border-strip to Canada, avoiding the craters, going neither too fast nor too slow.

24

THE TREES GOT BIGGER and farther apart. The road was wide and straight: two lanes of fine white gravel with a deep ditch on either side. They switched drivers without slowing down. Williams set the Chrysler on 65. Crystal opened the glove compartment and unfolded the old map that had been wrapped around the first owl. It stopped at the U.S. border. They were in unknown territory now.

Williams almost passed the store before he saw it. It was a two-story log building in a clearing bulldozed out of the trees. There was no sign but there were two gas pumps out front. He pulled in.

"Hit says BP," Crystal said. "Think they'll take Moline?"

"I'm going to get the gas first and ask questions later," Williams said.

An old woman with rolled-up stockings and a French accent filled the tank, while Crystal got behind the wheel and Williams shopped inside the store. He picked out a few Paydays and Collie Bars, ginger snaps, a six-pack of Coke, a carton of Laredos. Laredos? Was that right?

There was no way to know. If he stared at it hard enough, even the familiar picture of the cowboy on the rail fence rolling a smoke looked strange.

"Comes to forty-six dollars American," the old woman said. "I don't take no Canadian."

Williams handed her the Moline card and was relieved when she didn't hand it right back. Was she going to let him charge it all? The cash register had a small TV screen. The old woman rang up forty-six dollars, then stuck the card into a slot. The screen lit up:

CHECKING THIS CARD FOR YOUR OWN PROTECTION

The screen went dark, then lit up again:

> ARMED AND DANGEROUS
> DO NOT ATTEMPT CAPTURE CARD
> PRESS "RETURN" TO ALERT POLICE

The woman stared at the screen and Williams realized she couldn't read English. "It says 'Your purchase profoundly appreciated and approved,'" he told her, holding out his hand.

She handed him the card and the slip to sign. Behind her the screen went dark, then lit up again:

EXCUSEZ LE DELAI

ARME ET DANGEREUX
N'ESSAYEZ PAS DE RECUPERER LA CARTE
PRESSEZ «RETURN» POUR ALERTER LA POLICE

Her back was still to the screen when Williams signed the slip and started out the door.

The cash register went "beep," and she turned and read the screen. She turned back to look at Williams in amazement.

"Armed and dangerous," he said.

She pressed RETURN and a bell outside began ringing. The cash drawer popped open. She pulled out a small black .32 automatic.

"It says 'armed and dangerous'!" Williams said.

She pointed the gun at his face and fired.

The glass in the door behind him shattered. The bell sounded louder.

Williams backed out the door. Behind him, he heard the car door slam and the engine start. There was another shot and he tripped and fell backward down the steps, candy bars and Cokes flying. He scooped up as much as he could and ran for the car, his shoulder blades pinched together, waiting for a bullet to slice in between them.

He looked back and saw the old lady aiming with both hands; he heard the boom of the .30-30 from the car and saw her jump back in the doorway.

Crystal was leaning across the seat, holding the right front door open, and the car was already moving. The rifle was on the front seat, smoking from every crack. Williams jumped in as Crystal hit the gas, showering the pumps and the store with gravel. The old woman was on the steps again, dodging gravel and shooting in every direction.

They were up to 65 in 11.5 seconds; the gravel was noisy but smooth as concrete. The cabin was quickly lost in the giant pines. There was nothing but moon and trees ahead.

"I'll never shop there again," said Williams. Crystal was grinning like crazy. He grinned back and tossed her a pack of Laredos, then threw the cookies and candy bars into the back seat—then he turned and looked again, startled.

Someone was asleep in the back seat.

It was Talking Man.

25

A MILE DOWN THE road they passed Hey Hoss's Dodge pickup. The windows and tires were all shot out. The radiator was still hissing steam. Williams winced as Crystal sped past without slowing.

"They were chasing Talking Man," Crystal said. "Now we're chasing them."

"Hey Hoss shot up his own truck?"

"They're not exactly Hey Hoss," Crystal said. "Talking Man says she can make people, then make them do crazy things."

"Like shoot up their own trucks?" It was weird but somehow no longer surprising.

The road lay straight as a spear pointed at the heart of the moon, through a forest that was at the same time thin and tall, like a balding man's long hair. The trees were all the same kind: straight limbless pines, two feet thick and a hundred feet high. There was no brush on the forest floor and no clouds in the sky, only the occasional northeast-southwest scratch of a vapor trail.

Crystal liked these woods. They were clean and neat, unlike the tangled brushy woods down south. They reminded her of a two-page picture in her science book taken a hundred million years ago, when there was only one kind of plant and one kind of animal.

Williams didn't like the woods. They were too thin. The air was too cool and dry. It rustled in his lungs like dead leaves when he breathed.

"So, where'd he come from?" Williams asked.

"He was hiding in the woods."

"So now we can head back," Williams said.

"We have to keep going. They were chasing him. Now we're chasing them. They have the jar, the . . . unbeen. We have to beat them to the city, Edminidine."

"Ed what?"

"The North Pole."

"Let's don't and say we did."

"We can't go back anyway," Crystal said. "We'll get shot."

"We can find another road."

"Have you seen any other roads?"

"Then we can pull over and wait."

"Wait for what?"

"Wait for Talking Man to wake up, then figure out what the hell is going on."

"He's not asleep; he's . . . dreaming. Can't you hear him singing?"

Williams could hear him singing.

"He says we're going home."

"Bullshit," Williams said. It seemed to him like a million years since he had gotten off the parkway at Morgantown. He wished the rock hadn't hit his windshield.

"He says this is the way home."

"How can this be the way home when home is that way?"

"He says the world is not the only thing that's round."

Williams didn't answer.

"Okay?"

"Okay, okay."

They switched drivers without slowing down and shared the last of the Collie Bars and a Coke and the last of the ginger snaps. Even though he was mad at her, Crystal sat close to Williams, homesick in this hall of high trees. It got dark and she went to sleep and the radio came on. Williams tried to find a station while Crystal slept with her head on his lap, the honey-colored light from the radio all over her hair. There was nothing but static. Now he felt homesick too. They were off the map.

The moon was bright now, with an ice cap at its upper pole. Reddish clouds swirled around the equator; lights in the south went on, then off, like cities under fast-moving clouds.

The road narrowed gradually and the trees flashed by as Williams set the Chrysler on 60 and bored into the endless radio-empty northward-leading car-lighted tunnel of night. It was better than trying to sleep.

26

SCRUMP. WHUMP. There was a whack as a rock hit the bottom of the Chrysler. Williams slowed to 45. Another rock hit and the radio went dark. Crystal sat up.

"What was that?"

Nothing, she was told. Talking Man dreamed on. Williams drove on. Crystal looked around. The road was changing. They were still in the trees, but the trees were smaller, and now she could see the sky, growing lighter, going to green like pond water. The trees were interrupted by long boggy stretches, with dead trees standing in them like leftover prehistoric animals. The road was rougher, covered with brown, heavy stones as big as eggs. There was a curve, the first since the border. Crystal lay back down with her head in Williams's lap and closed her eyes. The land began to roll

like a river after a towboat goes by. Williams smoothed
her hair behind her ears . . . then realized the radio
was off completely.

"Don't stop. That feels nice," she said.

"I thought you were asleep."

"I don't think I've been asleep at all. I've been
dreaming."

"You can't dream without sleeping."

"Sure you can, I think. I think I've been dreaming
Talking Man's dream."

"Which is?" Williams wasn't sure he really wanted to
know.

"He was dreaming he was talking to me."

"I thought he always talked to you. He talked to you
the first day I met you."

"Just about business. Since my mother died. Not
about stuff like this."

"Which is?" Williams definitely wasn't sure he really
wanted to know.

But he could tell she wanted to talk. . . .

Time is like a rope, encircling all things, Crystal said
Talking Man said. If we drive far enough north, every
direction will be south. Even the future will be past.
We'll come to Edminidine.

Like a robe?

Like a rope.

Tell me this: Who is the woman in the white car?

His . . . his . . . She didn't know what to call her.
Dgene, who used to be with him in Elennor, where
they dreamed the dream that was the world . . . until
he fell in love with hit and took the owl and came to
live with my mother, in the trailer, where I was born.

He ran away?

Because the end of time is cold and lonely, and the moon is just rings—a junk planet in the sky—and the sky itself is just a junkyard of wrecked stars.

Because my mother had those narrow, uplooking mountain eyes even when she was looking down, she said he told her.

They met at a fish fry on the Barren River, down among the sycamores, the giraffe-barked sycamores; Williams could see the sycamores in Crystal's mind's eye as clear as the words of a song. Her mother's name was Laurel Ann; musical stage name, Mountain Laurel. Between the trees, the ground was as clean as a park.

Then you were born.

Crystal's ear blushed under his fingertips. Aren't you leaving something out?

You know what I mean. Anyway.

Anyway. Crystal sat up and lit a cigarette, then lay back down.

He said not to worry about my tobacco, she said.

Tell me this: Is this the real owl? Williams took it out of the glove compartment. It was cold in its plastic bag.

Hit is now. Now there are three. Once there was only one. He bought another just like hit, to fool her, from a souvenir store in Nashville.

That's the one he kept on top of the TV set.

To trick her he planned. But she used hit to follow him to the real one he had hidden, he imagined (foolishly, she said) forever, in the oil pan of a '50 Ford in Owensboro.

I thought it was a '49. That was the real owl, then?

Then. Except, now, they all are real. Even the one you are holding that never was supposed to exist before.

What do you mean never supposed to exist before?

He says that's what the world does. Hit makes things real, whether you want them to be or not.

Williams put the owl back and closed the glove compartment door.

So tell me this: What does the owl do if we get to where we're going?

Hit keeps the stuff she has from coming through.

What stuff?

In the jar.

I mean, what's it called?

The unbeen.

That's not a name.

Hit doesn't have a name. How could hit?

And if we don't beat her there?

Hit will go through, back into time.

And if we beat her?

Hit won't, I guess.

Then we what?

Then we go home.

Then we go home?

Then we go home.

The radio light came on.

When Crystal woke up, it was daylight and the trees were gone. They were in open country covered with long grass. The sun was low. The road was crossing a low ridge, down into a shallow, marshy valley. In the backseat Talking Man was sitting up, awake. At the bottom of the hill, the road ended.

There was a log-and-plywood bridge over a narrow stream. Beyond the stream there was a hillside of tall grass—and no road.

Two big white dogs were drinking from the stream.

They looked up as the car approached, showing themselves by their necklaces to be wolves. They splashed through the water and disappeared into the tall grass on the other side.

Williams stopped at the bridge: two logs covered with standard five-by-seven plywood sheets. It was the first sign of civilization (except for the road itself) since the old woman with the gun. On the earth, that is, of course. On the moon there were mysterious lights; and in the sky were vapor trails, usually in sets of two.

While the car was idling and Williams was wondering what to do, a road appeared. A set of tracks, like the trace of a ghost car driving through the grass, was moving up the hill. It was halfway, then higher.

Crystal pointed, but Williams had already seen it. Without bothering to think, he followed. The plywood boomed as the Chrysler rolled across and then plunged into the tall grass. The ground felt wet, so Williams kept the speed up to 10, but no faster.

He didn't want to catch up with whatever it was he was following.

The tracks reached the top of the hill—and the two wolves stepped out of the grass, side by side, onto the gray stone. Both were white with black feet. They looked back, then disappeared down the other side of the hill, staying exactly 5.5 feet apart.

When the Chrysler reached the top, Williams stopped again and shut off the engine this time. They all got out, even Talking Man. They could see in every direction for a long way. Far behind, they could see the dark line of the forest that encircles that world like a robe. Crystal shivered, and Williams put his arm around her shoulders. Ahead they saw a dry sea. And far across it, they saw taillights flash.

27

IT WAS LIGHT BUT there was no sun. From the bottom of the hill, the dry sea stretched north until it became the horizon. The giant moon hung over it like a smoky lamp. The gently sloping sea floor of gray cracked mud was smooth and clean, as if it had died long before it had dried up.

To the east and north, the sea went on forever; to the west, it was entwined in long curves with the arms of the land. The arms of the sea were dark gray; the arms of the land were light gray, littered with rock.

The two wolves were trotting north and west along the shoreline, still 5.5 feet apart. Far ahead of them on the same rocky beach, taillights flashed. Williams tried, but he couldn't make out the car.

Crystal drove down the hill. Williams sat beside her,

tired of driving but not tired enough to sleep. Talking Man, through with singing, sat in the back seat and smoked. The beach was sloped and the Chrysler slanted to the right as Crystal eased it up to speed, looping in and out of the long, shallow bays, following the shoreline north and west. She passed the wolves after two miles. The beach was fairly smooth, but 55 was tops because of the slant and the long curves; and Crystal had to brake every few minutes for boulders or washouts. Now she knew why the taillights had flashed on the other car.

Williams lay down and went to sleep. Talking Man sat straight up in the back, and even though she couldn't see his face, Crystal knew he looked worried. She knew why. At this rate, they would never catch up with the other car.

Then she got an idea.

The beach curved west, but she went straight, north, down, onto the ocean floor, the dry mud crackling under her wheels like fire.

70, 80, 90, 100.

Williams dreamed he was listening to the radio. Chuck Berry was singing "Maybelline," but it was in Russian and the radio was on fire. He woke up in a cold sweat. Something was wrong.

His head was on Crystal's lap, and looking up he saw the comforting shape of her breasts from below, and beyond them her face, looking tense but wild but pleased. The wind was screaming. There was a nasty crackling noise like fire. It was dark, and the dashboard lights were on.

Williams sat up.

The speedometer was on 112.

They were in the center of the dry sea.

Ahead and behind, he could see nothing but mud and darkness. Far to the west, he could barely make out the white sand shoreline. All the windows were rolled up, and when he reached over to open one, Talking Man shook his head. Of course not, not at 112. Williams looked at Crystal, and she grinned. He tried to grin back. He had never gone this fast before. Much less with a girl driving.

Talking Man tapped the window and pointed. On the dark shoreline to the left, taillights flashed, then flashed again, falling behind.

Crystal managed to wring a few more turns out of the 413. 116, 118. The speedometer was pegged at 120, but the Chrysler was still picking up speed after the other car's lights were long gone far behind.

An hour later they switched drivers without slowing down. They had been cruising at 115. The temperature was holding steady. Williams had worried about the gas, but it was at almost half a tank, going up, not down. Crystal's foot came off the gas a second too soon, and the Chrysler began to swap ends, but Williams brought the car back into line and up to speed while he slipped under her into the driver's seat. They were getting good. He had never gone so fast before, and like Crystal, he grinned. He ran the Chrysler back up to 120, then back down to 115, cruising into the night, for it was night, even though the night was brighter than the day.

The mud was beginning to slope upward slightly. Ahead was the ocean's end, the shoreline, and beyond it a low range of hills, all ghostly in the moonlight.

Williams hit the beach at 60, then slowed to 40, looking for a way north through the hills. There was no road, but the stone seemed smooth enough to cross. He headed up into a notch between the hills, the Chrysler rocking, the torsion bars creaking. Now the top speed was 15. At the top of the pass, Crystal and Talking Man looked back, but there was no sign of the other car.

"So we beat them?" Williams asked. "What does that mean?"

"Hit means we get to the city first," Crystal said. "We close the passage between the end of time and the beginning before they let the unbeen through."

"I wonder why they didn't head across the mud too?"

Crystal looked back at Talking Man, then said, "He says maybe hit's still water to her."

North of the pass, it was slow going—35 on the flat lakebeds, 15 on the rocky gravel washes, 5 to 10 across the hills. The land looked like it had been hosed down and dried off. They wound their way north, following the moon. There was no more grass or brush, just an occasional green smear of moss on a rock. Talking Man and Crystal both slept. The radio was on, but there was nothing on it, not even static; it seemed as empty as the spaces between the stars.

Williams drove as slowly and steadily as he could. He had heard too many stories of torsion bars heating up, then snapping like wire when they were rocked too long on rough country roads.

But what went was not the suspension.

There was something on the radio.

Williams thought he heard singing, but he couldn't get it to come in. There was low talk, like a talk show, and a woman's laugh. As he adjusted the dial, he heard a snap and an ugly rattle that sounded like engine parts coming loose.

He turned the radio off.

It was quiet, and the 413 was running as smoothly as ever. He turned the radio back on. There was a wild clatter, like a rock in a can, then the laugh again. It was the woman's laugh. He turned the radio off. There was another clatter, definitely from the engine this time, then silence. Williams coasted to a stop and listened to the idle, as smooth as silk—

Except that the oil pressure was zero.

He shut the engine off.

Talking Man and Crystal both sat up.

"I think the oil pump just broke."

Crystal's eyes grew wide with horror. Talking Man made a twisting motion with his thumb and finger, to the right. Williams started the car and leaned over so that Talking Man could see the oil pressure gauge, then shut if off again when Talking Man nodded.

"I think she broke it," Williams said.

Talking Man got out of the car and looked around at the low barren hills in four directions. Then he got into the front seat, making Crystal scoot over, and pointed to a low spot on the ridge to the right. Williams started the car and drove up the slope as gently as possible. The 413 was smooth and quiet, but driving was torture. If he ran it hard, the oil-starved engine would seize; if he ran it very long, even at idle, it would seize. His skin crawled, waiting for the titanic whack whack whack of a thrown rod.

From the top of the hill, the land sloped down to a long, narrow dry lakebed facing east. At the near end of it, where it had come to rest among the stones, was an ancient silver Air France Lockheed Constellation airliner.

Talking Man made the twisting motion with his thumb and finger, this time to the left. Williams cut off the engine and rolled down the rocky hillside. With the power steering off, the Chrysler handled like an old John Deere.

28

POWERED BY FOUR MASSIVE eighteen-cylinder Wright Cyclone engines, the Lockheed 749 was one of the most successful of the piston-engine long-range airliners. With its gracefully drooping fuselage, it suggested today's supersonic Concorde and is still considered one of the most beautiful piston-engine airliners ever built. The 749A Constellation, of which 233 were built, had a cruising speed of 327 knots at 21,000 feet and was sold to TWA, Air France, KLM, and other major intercontinental airlines. One was lost over Brooklyn, New York, in a spectacular collision; another was lost over the savannah of western Africa, where foxes today nest in its long bones; and another on a flight over the North Pole.

Talking Man said there was a small camshaft-driven

gear, Crystal said, under the distributor drive of the late-model Cyclone 3350, that would fit the oil pump drive gear in the Chrysler 413. All they had to do was pull it out and put it in.

The plane lay on its belly at the bottom of the hill. One wing was bent, but both were still attached. One engine had broken loose and lay smashed in a pile of boulders all its own size, where it looked like another version of them; the others were still attached to the wings. It had been a crash landing rather than a crash, and if Williams squinted a little to soften the smashed propeller blades and crumpled wing tips, he could almost imagine that the plane had just touched down to pick up a passenger or two and would fly away again.

The right (starboard) inboard engine was the easiest to get to. Williams watched, ready to help, as Talking Man began to tear the engine down. The cowling was held on by rivets, which Talking Man popped off with a screwdriver. Then there was a radiatorlike cooler held on with $3/8$-inch bolts. Under this was an aluminum bracket secured on both sides of the engine by $7/16$-inch bolts. Williams held out his hand to indicate that he could help. After hesitating for only a moment, Talking Man searched through his pockets and found a $7/16$-inch socket and driver for him. They loosened the bracket, Talking Man tossing each bolt as he removed it into the gravelly sand. This was a junkyard habit that bothered Williams. He put the bolts in his pocket, even though he knew they would never be putting the Wright engine back together again.

Under the bracket, there was a copper fuel line. The fitting was too tight to crack with an open end wrench, and Talking Man began to rummage in the pockets of his sport coat again. Williams figured he was looking for vise-grips. When he pulled out a Little Jewel line-cutter, the small one that is in every transmission man's toolbox, Williams realized that the old man's jacket pockets were deep indeed. Next there was a housing supporting the rocker bearings, and Talking Man handed Williams a half-inch socket and an extension, and they worked together, each on a different side of the engine. Williams got used to tossing bolts on the ground more easily than he'd thought he would.

Meanwhile, Crystal was exploring the inside of the airliner.

When she was six, she had gone with her mother back home to Newport, Tennessee, at the foot of the Smoky Mountains, and the inside of the plane reminded her of her Aunt Eula's 1951 Buick Roadmaster. Everything was narrow and dark, decorated with swirly wood and gray velour. The seats were plush with maple armrests. The windows were small and round. Everyone in the crash must have gotten away, for there were no bodies or even bloodstains. Crystal had been afraid there would be skeletons staring out the windows.

In a rack in the front, there were magazines. They looked like the *Saturday Evening Post*s and *Look*s at her Aunt Eula's, with pictures of families and new cars and appliances in the ads. The father always wore a hat. The mother was always smiling and the boy was always older than the girl. The only difference was, they were in French.

The gear was keyed on a shaft; Talking Man tapped it off and caught the moon-shaped key, the only thing so far that he hadn't thrown away. He held it up and nodded. Williams gathered up his tools and headed for the car. He got the jack out of the trunk so they could jack up the front of the Chrysler and pull the oil pan to replace the oil pump gear. But Talking Man shook his head. Of course. If he could float a car in the air, why bother with a jack? Feeling foolish, Williams put the jack back into the trunk. But instead of lifting up the car, Talking Man opened the hood.

In the back of the plane there was a galley, but all the food was gone; Crystal wondered what had happened to the people. Had they taken it with them? Seeing the empty shelves, she realized she hadn't eaten or felt hungry since the old woman with the gun. Like the car, they were all running on empty. She found some little twin-packs of crackers like the ones they give away with soup in restaurants, but they were so stale she could bend them through the cellophane.

She heard a faraway, familiar sound. Was that a car? She bent down and looked out a porthole. Williams and Talking Man were working on the Chrysler. The sound came from the other side of the gravel hill, and as Crystal listened, it faded away. On the ridgetop, she saw one of the two white wolves looking down, then turning and trotting off, north. For some reason, the sight made her immensely sad.

Talking Man and Williams worked on.

After searching through his pockets for a cigarette—like Crystal, he could always find one—Talking Man pulled the Chrysler's distributor cap and began to disconnect the smaller wires. Williams watched, amazed. He wasn't going to pull the oil pan at all. He was going to try and replace the gear from the top, through the distributor shaft hole.

Talking Man pulled the distributor and laid it across the intake manifold. Then he motioned for Williams to get into the car. While he peered down into the narrow hole, he held his thumb and one finger together and turned them to the right twice; Williams bumped the starter twice, then once more. Talking Man pulled a rawhide shoelace out of his pocket and fed it down into the hole. When he pulled it out a half a gear was stuck to it. He shook it once and the gear dropped into the gravel. He twisted his fingers to the right once more, and Williams bumped the starter again. Talking Man straightened the shoelace and fished out the other half of the gear.

Talking Man laid the new gear from the Wright engine next to the hole and looked at it thoughtfully. Williams could see what the problem was. Half gears would come out, but the hole was too small for the new gear to go down—even if a way was found to get it on the shaft after it was inside the engine.

Talking Man spit on the gear and rubbed it with his thumb. He tried it in the hole, but it still wouldn't fit. He spit on it again.

The curved side door of the airliner opened. Williams came in.

"Any luck?"

"We found it," Williams said. "I guess it's the right gear. He got it in. He's hooking up the distributor right now."

"Well then?"

Williams grinned. "Your old man's pretty good. He

fixed the oil pump without pulling the pan. From the top. I never thought anybody could do that."

"He does hit with magic. Hit's not as hard as hit looks."

"Still."

"I guess this means we go on," Crystal said, looking dejected.

"I thought that's what you always wanted."

"Williams."

"What?"

"Do you think we'll ever get home?"

"I thought you were the one who always wanted to keep going," he said, cruelly. "I quit worrying about it."

"Oh, never mind." Crystal looked out the window of the airplane. There was nothing out there but stones. She wished the car hadn't broken, then she wished they hadn't fixed it. She felt like crying or at least not trying not to anymore.

Williams started to put his arms around her. But the dim, narrow aisle was like the aisle of a movie theatre, and he kept expecting somebody to tell him to sit down. Crystal looked up at him, and he stepped back nervously so he could see her better.

"What's in this old airplane?" he said, craning his neck to look around.

"Nothing."

"Not even one skeleton?" He went up and tried the cockpit door, which was locked. There was a smell that might have been a skeleton. When he came back, she had her feet across the aisle.

"Toll bridge," she said.

They had never kissed before, and in fact, Crystal

had never kissed any boy. After a while, she stuck her tongue in his mouth to see what it was like. Her breasts felt tingly with no bra. They kissed again, and then came that unexpected sweet moment, when a boy puts his hand under a girl's sweater and instead of stopping him she lets him go ahead, nipple and fingertip touching, surprising them both.

"Crystal . . ." he started to say. She looked around.

There was a sound outside.

The car starting.

29

THE TOP OF THE world is not ice and snow, as is generally believed, but a city of seamless stone, as colorless as unfired pottery, sprawling across the flat, featureless pole between low, unsteep ranges of hills. The city is all made of identical square one-story gray buildings, each with one window and one door in the same wall. Built but never used for a million million years, it was already waiting when the moon was first captured by the earth, still waiting when it was shattered into rings, and it has waited ever since, with no roads leading in or out.

Then, one day, two cars came, a half an hour apart, both approaching from the low ridges to the south.

Of course, from Edminidine, every direction is south.

*   *   *

Williams drove. The moon had set while they had been at the airliner, and there was still no sun, but it was lighter than before: A cold glow filled the sky from behind sheets of paper-colored clouds to the west. Talking Man slept folded up in the back seat like a rag doll, greasy from fixing the car. Crystal dozed against the door. Williams made sure the radio was off and left it off.

The gas gauge still sat between a quarter and a half. It had quit going up, but it wasn't going down. The oil pressure was fine.

Williams drove what he assumed to be north, but without the moon there no way of knowing for sure. He kept the clouds to his left. There was no trace of a road and no trace of the other car, but he figured it must have passed them while they were broken down. Williams steered the Chrysler along the bottoms of the shallow valleys, stones covered with stones, winding up and around the ridgetops when the valleys ended, and then only until he could descend to another one. He didn't like the ridgetops: You could see too far, and as far as you could see it was the same low, gravelly hills.

Then he crossed the last hill, a hill just like all the others, and saw the lightless city filling the plain below. He stopped and put the car into park but didn't shut it off. He looked for the center of town, but it was all the same, with no place to focus his eyes. The edges of the city just sort of dwindled off into gray rocks.

Crystal sat up. "Edminidine."

There was a rustling in the back seat like old paper. Talking Man sat up. He searched through his pockets and managed to find a cigarette, which he straightened and shared with Crystal as Williams drove slowly down the hill and into the city.

There were no streets, just the spaces between the buildings, which all faced different directions. Williams tried to keep the brightening sky to his left as he drove between the clay-colored buildings. Every turn forced him to go left, and he felt like he was going in circles; but the sky spun with him, so he felt he was always going north. Talking Man and Crystal smoked and looked out the window, saying nothing. The deeper into the city Williams drove, the closer together the buildings got, until finally the Chrysler could go no farther without going back.

He stopped. He looked toward the backseat. Talking Man made a leftward twisting motion with his thumb and forefinger, and Williams switched the engine off.

Talking Man pointed at the glove compartment, and Crystal opened it and took out the owl. Even in its plastic bag it was too cold to carry, so she put it in a paper bag and rolled the top over into a handle.

They all got out. The closing of the car doors sounded like thunder, but it was quickly gone. A great silence ate every sound.

Talking Man held his head cocked to one side. He seemed to be sniffing the air. Crystal watched him, hunching her shoulders against the cold, holding the paper bag by the top like a purse. Williams took off his Levi jacket and put it around her shoulders.

Talking Man found an Iver Johnson .32 automatic in one pocket and a clip in the other. He slid the clip into the gun with a booming click and slid the gun back into his pocket.

Talking Man started walking. Crystal followed him, taking two steps to his one. Williams followed the two of them, but Talking Man stopped, shook his head and pointed back at the car.

Williams sat on the hood of the car and waited, he didn't know what for. It was the first time he'd been alone in days. All around was silence. The only sound was the ticking of the cooling engine under the warm hood. He looked around. The empty window and door frames on the buildings were all the same size, as if they had been fitted for one giant order of glass and doors that had never been delivered.

The city looked weird in the half light, half dark. Williams slid off the car and walked to one of the doors and looked in. He saw only a bare, square room. There was no dirt, no junk, no leftover building materials.

The others were the same.

The walls were something that wasn't quite stone and wasn't quite plastic. Williams ran his fingers across one, and it felt like a blackboard.

He sat back on the hood of the car. The heat felt good on the backs of his legs. He wished he smoked. It would at least be something to do. He wished he had something to eat. He wished he had a gun.

Then he remembered that he did have a gun.

He got the old Winchester "yellowboy" out of the back seat and jacked out the last two shells. Snick snack, snick snack. It was the loudest noise in the whole city. He reloaded the rifle and held it across his lap. To the west, the sunset sky was getting lighter.

He decided to look around some more.

He walked in the direction Talking Man and Crystal had gone. Was it north? The streets turned left, then left again. Williams counted his steps so he wouldn't get lost. He turned a corner and thought for a second that he was going in circles, for there was a car in front of him—a two-door hardtop at that.

But it was the mystery car, not the Chrysler.

He put a shell in the chamber of the Winchester and walked closer. It was the first time he'd had a good look at the car since Owensboro. From the front, it looked like a Ford, with a toothy grille. From the back it had that Chrysler products' swoopy look. The sides were sculptured like a Buick. He looked inside. There were McDonald's wrappers and Dixie cups on the floor in the back and an opened, half-empty box of Western shotgun shells on the back seat. There was a box of Kleenex on the front seat.

Williams looked around, then tried the door, but it was locked.

He wanted revenge for the Mustang. He felt like putting a shot through the windshield, but it wasn't the car's fault. He would have at least slit the tires, but the Buck knife was in his Levi jacket, with Crystal wearing it. He squatted down and opened a valve with his thumbnail to let the air out. It was a slow business. The hissing was now the loudest noise in town, until suddenly he heard a louder one, a deep scraping noise that came up through his boots and hurt his bones.

He stood up.

He heard a shot.

Then another.

Then, long and high, more painful than anything he had ever heard or even imagined before, a scream.

30

FOLLOWING TALKING MAN THROUGH the narrowing streets, Crystal wondered what would happen when the buildings got too close together to walk between. She had to hurry to keep up with him. She found the hurrying feeling comforting. It reminded her of going to the stock car races in Owensboro a long time ago. All the other cars had to wait in line, but the officials just waved Talking Man's 1950 Ford on through. There was a number on the door of the car, and she was the little girl in the front seat, looking back at everybody as they drove through the gate. It was getting lighter, or was it her imagination? The sky was milky gray, not dark enough for stars and not light enough for shadows. The streets seemed to get wide again. They were approaching the center of the city.

Talking Man stopped.

Crystal bumped into him, almost dropping the bag with the owl.

All of a sudden she could hear the immense silence all around and she was scared. No wind. No breathing. Not even footsteps. Talking Man took one step and she followed.

Another step.

She turned a corner and something darted across her path and she jumped back.

It was her shadow.

Crystal looked behind her. Something was coming up, but it wasn't the sun. It wasn't the moon either. It was big, and it sparkled like a wheel of jewels encircling the world. She started to say something, but Talking Man's gasoline-smelling hand clamped over her mouth. His other hand on her shoulder pulled her down beside him. He was crouched at the corner of a house.

They were at the center of the city.

Ahead, in the new light, Crystal could see an open square with a low circular fountain at the center of it.

Dgene had beaten them. She was standing at the edge of the fountain, her white dress shimmering in the new light, rippling almost as if there had been a wind. She was holding the Mason jar, trying to unscrew the lid. The man in the blue STP vest was standing beside her with the short shotgun under his arm. He looked like Hey Hoss, only fatter. Crystal had never realized before that Dgene was beautiful. The light from the newly risen rings made her face and hair sparkle.

She tapped the jar lid against the side of the fountain, then tried it again. Now Crystal could feel Talking

Man's fear in his hand on her arm. This was the well between the worlds. This was the horror Dgene had come to release, the unbeen. The jar lid moved; as it turned, it made a noise like mountains moving over.

Scared, Crystal reached for Talking Man's hand, but he was gone, running toward Dgene. He had taken the paper bag from her hand, and suddenly she was alone.

She had never seen him move so fast before.

Dgene held the jar above her head, but Talking Man jumped so high he would have gotten it easily if the man in the STP vest hadn't blown him out of the air with a shotgun blast that sent him spinning like a rag doll into the side of the fountain at the woman's bare feet.

The jar fell. It hit the stones of the square but didn't break, and rolled into the new shadows. Jumping over Talking Man's body, Dgene ran after it.

Crystal ran to Talking Man, but she couldn't take her eyes off the jar; now it was unscrewing by itself with that awful noise. Dgene stood over it, waiting. Crystal remembered the gun and found it in Talking Man's coat pocket, but all of a sudden she didn't want to shoot Dgene, who was shining like a fairy in the ring-light.

Instead, she shot the man in the blue vest.

He put his hand to his gut and stumbled backward and sat down on the fountain edge; she shot him again and he fell backward. His screams got louder and farther away at the same time, for he had fallen and would fall forever into the well between the worlds.

Crystal knelt back down by Talking Man. He was crumpled up on the cold stones. The side of his coat was shot full of holes, but he wasn't bleeding. His right arm was flapping. He was trying to throw the bag with the owl into the fountain, but his arm wouldn't throw; it just flapped horribly. Crystal started to cry. Quit crying he told her and throw it. What? Throw it, he said to her, into the well, and it will close forever; miss it and the unbeen will feed on the stars themselves, for there is no end to its hunger. Crystal picked up the bag and pulled back to throw it, but something grabbed her arm. She yelled. It was the small cowboy with the rat mustache. He looked like Hey Hoss only skinnier. He grabbed at her breast, and that made her mad. But it was the Buck knife he was after. She had never known you could open one with one hand. Then it looked like he was holding up heaven with the tip of the blade touching the glistening newly risen rings. Crystal screamed when she saw the point coming down, and she held up her hand. That made it hurt twice as bad, first as it pierced her palm and then as it pierced her heart, and she fell backward onto Talking Man.

A flap opened just above the cowboy's left eye and a warm, reddish spray came out all over her. Crystal heard a shot.

She heard a howling.

31

MEANWHILE THE JAR LID quit turning and fell off. Nothing came out and kept on coming. Dgene reached toward it and pulled her arm back. Her hand was gone. She examined her wrist, turning it, looking for it. The unbeen was slick like water and sticky like fire, and it rolled out of the jar and kept coming. And kept coming.

Dgene was like a child out of breath: her mouth open but no sound coming out. By the time her scream reached the world, the unbeen was as big as a car, and she was standing in it.

32

THE UNBEEN WAS SLICK like water and sticky like fire. It was the first thing Williams saw after he shot the cowboy. It rolled, feeding on itself, toward Dgene, crackling as it lapped around her bare feet. She fell folding as her feet dissolved. Her scream was not exactly a scream of pain. Her feet were gone, her arms that had caught her were short sticks. She scrambled to her knees and her knees were gone; she slid down on one disappearing side trying very hard to scream, but now there was nothing there to make the sound: no lungs, no throat, just her open mouth and eyes and the unbeen rolling over her, rolling over her. She was a dark shape in the car-sized clear liquid, then just a shadow. Two spots took longer to dissolve. They stared out at Williams like victims of a fire watching the crowd watch them burn.

Williams ran to Crystal.

The cowboy had fallen on top of her. Williams rolled him over. He looked like Hey Hoss, only skinnier. Blood was oozing from the mouth-size hole over his eye.

Crystal looked dead. She was stabbed in the heart and she looked dead. Williams pulled the Buck knife out and skipped it across the stones like a rock. He tried to pick her up, but she was too heavy. He put his ear to her lips, but he felt no breathing. Then Williams heard Talking Man breathing. His breath sounded like the wind scraping. Leave her here with me, he said, and Williams was scared because he had never heard him talk before, the words coming not through his ears but somewhere behind his eyes like the singing.

Go close the jar, he said, before the unbeen comes out forever.

Williams looked behind him. The unbeen was still coming out of the jar, rolling toward the well in the center of the square.

Williams walked to the edge of the well and looked over, still holding the Winchester. It was like looking up into the sky at night. The stars that he hadn't seen in a month were all down there. There was a deep howling, and he couldn't turn his eyes away.

Go close the jar Talking Man sang.

Williams laid the rifle down and ran across the square. The clear stuff flowed out in a never-ending stream. He was afraid to touch the jar, but he had to. It was cold, cold, cold. He found the lid and picked it up. His hand brushed the unbeen, and the tips of two fingers were gone. As if they had never been. There was a cold feeling worse than pain, because it didn't hurt, but they were gone.

Close the jar.

Williams screwed the lid on the jar. Cut off from the jar, the unbeen on the stones seemed to thicken. It turned from the well and rolled toward Talking Man and Crystal. Talking Man pushed the cowboy toward it with his feet, and the stuff rolled over the cowboy with a crackling sound. He was gone. It kept rolling, and Talking Man crawled between it and Crystal. It licked at him.

Williams ran to get the rifle. Talking Man pulled himself up on one disappearing elbow and threw the owl toward the howling well, because if the owl went through, the well between the worlds would be closed, but if the unbeen got through, it would eat the stars.

He missed.

The owl bounced off the rim of the fountain and rolled toward the unbeen.

Williams dove for it, for what would happen if the unbeen ate it?

He must have missed. He hit the rim and must have fallen through. The howling was all around. He must have missed and fallen through, for there were a million million miles of stars in every direction.

33

THE BLOOD ON THE side of Williams's face was dried, and it pulled at his cheek when he opened his eyes. He looked around, trying to remember where he was, not in any hurry to find out. He rubbed his eyes, and his hand felt funny. He looked at it: all the fingers on his right hand were the same length, and the two center ones had no nails. They just ended. He felt curiously indifferent, as if they had always been that way.

Now he remembered. Looking up, he saw the rings that had once been the moon, lighted now like a jeweled wheel across the sky.

How long had he lain here?

He stood up. He was in the fountain at the center of the square. The howling distances, the stars, were gone; it was just a dusty fountain, dried up except for a big wet spot near the wall.

The owl was nowhere to be seen.

Talking Man and Crystal lay in a heap against the fountain wall, Crystal cradled in her father's arm. Williams heard snoring.

It was Crystal.

He ran over.

There was blood all over her sweatshirt, and it was torn. He pulled it up before he remembered she wasn't wearing a bra; but she didn't notice anyway. There were two scars on the top of her left breast where one had been before. They were matched like a snakebite mark. Both were completely healed.

Talking Man was bleeding. He was alive, but barely. There was only half of him left. His right leg was bent under him at an impossible angle. His left arm and most of his left leg were missing where he had rolled into the unbeen. But he was conscious, and he pointed across the little square with his right hand. Williams saw the jar, lying on its side, filled with a thick liquid that looked like moonshine.

Williams didn't want to pick it up, but Talking Man pointed again. The jar was cold and heavy. Williams made sure the lid was on tight. Talking Man nodded and pointed south, and Williams understood. He wanted Williams to take it home with him. He set it beside the "yellowboy," which was leaning against the fountain.

Talking Man seemed to be having trouble breathing. He raised up on what was left of one shoulder, looking through his pockets with his one hand. He finally found a pack of Laredos and handed them to Williams before falling back down, exhausted. The pack was sticky; Williams managed to find one cigarette and light it with Oh-Kay Motel matches from Crystal's jeans pocket. How long ago and far away that night seemed!

Talking Man took a deep drag, then pointed to Crystal. Williams had been thinking the same thing.

Williams had been worried about finding the Chrysler again, but it was no problem.

Either the car was closer or Crystal was lighter or he was stronger than before. Or all three. Williams wiped the blood off her face and put her into the front seat, asleep. He wondered how he was going to get Talking Man into the back. He wasn't looking forward to carrying him all by himself.

He looked, but there was no sign of the other car as he walked back to the square. The rings overhead were growing dimmer. Low fast dark clouds were moving in.

The car was definitely closer. Talking Man was still finishing his cigarette. "Did the stuff eat the owl?" Williams asked. "Or did the owl eat the stuff?" But there was no answer. He hadn't expected any. Things were back to normal.

Talking Man stubbed out his cigarette, then pointed to the rifle and the jar.

"You first," Williams said. He was going to have to make two trips, one for the old man and one for the stuff.

Talking Man shook his head and kept pointing. Williams reached for the Mason jar. Talking Man shook his head. Williams picked up the gun. Talking Man nodded, then pointed at himself. He held his thumb and one finger together and twisted them to the left.

Williams finally understood what he wanted. He wanted to go home. He was glad Crystal wasn't there.

He felt something cold on his cheek. It was starting to snow.

34

WILLIAMS DROVE WHILE CRYSTAL slept. The way back was different from the way up. Gone were the great dry seas and long beaches that had made part of their trip so much like flying. Gone were the long grasses and the guide wolves. Now there was a road. It wasn't paved, but it was graded and smooth enough to let the Chrysler make a steady 45. It led straight across a boulder-strewn plain, then wound among gravelly hills. Williams was tired, but there was nothing to do but push on. The Chrysler was back down to a quarter of a tank and slowly dropping. Williams was getting hungry, but there was nothing to eat. The snow filled the air but never stuck, as though it were always just starting. Williams had to drive with the headlights on. He couldn't tell night from day. Crystal slept and slept, but the radio wouldn't play. When Williams was too tired to drive anymore, he pulled over and curled up against Crystal and slept until the cold woke him up, then drove some more.

He wasn't about to sleep with the engine running and the heater on. He'd heard too many stories about teenage carbon monoxide parking disasters.

He wondered if the world was still changing.

The snow was still falling, but it was lighter, when the radio came on. Dim and remote, it was Dickie Lee singing "Nine Million, Nine Hundred Ninety-Nine Thousand, Nine Hundred Ninety-Nine Tears to Go," and it made home seem closer. At the same time, there was a soft, welcome womanly stirring against Williams's side, and Crystal rubbed her eyes and slowly stretched and went back to sleep. The radio died. Williams tried the dials, puzzled. Now the radio was reversed and only worked when she was awake.

A little later, Williams saw his first tree, a twisted pine exactly the size of a man. There were ice-blue flowers on each side of the road. Crystal was awake again, and they made her think of her tobacco. She wondered if it was still summer in Kentucky. In the crumpled pack Talking Man had given Williams, she managed to find a cigarette.

She had already looked in the backseat for Talking Man, but she wasn't surprised when he wasn't there; she didn't ask where he'd gone, and she didn't cry—until now, fumbling around the dashboard for a match.

Crystal was driving and the Chrysler was sitting on empty when they came to their first gas station, a log and sheetrock shed overlooking an unpaved superhighway heading south. Indian children filled the car by hand from lard tins, while adults gathered around to watch, for Chryslers were unusual here in the nation of the Dine. Inside the station, a TV blazed like a fire.

As they drove south, the snow turned to rain, and there were fields of barley between the all-the-same trees; then fields of dark green hay. Near the greatest of the Great Lakes, Tecumseh, there was even tobacco of a small (and, Crystal thought, sorry-looking) northern variety. They worked a day suckering it to buy gasoline and a yellow blouse for Crystal to wear under the Levi jacket that looked so drab here in the land of bright colors, the land the Wyandotte had saved with blood and fire.

Then south, through the spectacular gorges of the Wabash, into the flat, familiar corn belt country of the Illini, where babies watched from the trailer doors, too little and fat to wave. The Chrysler was no longer a curiosity, since there was one in every village here. The sun came out that day, and they camped for the night at the ferry landing on the bluffs across from Owensboro. When he saw Kentucky across the river, Williams's eyes filled with unexpected tears. He and Crystal watched the sky, hoping to see the awesome rings again, but all that came up was the moon, rising in the east, looking gorgeous but lifeless. They shared cornbread and beans and a Coke from a store; they bathed together in the muddy Ohio. That night, they made love for the first time, holding each other and talking until dawn. They were almost home.

Talking Man was right: He had told Crystal not to worry, that the neighbors would set her tobacco, and they had. Then had even suckered it once. Nobody had broken into the trailer. Williams tried the John

Deere, but although he got it to cough once or twice he never could get it started. Crystal and Williams spent one day plowing out the tobacco with Cleve Townsend's one-eared mule, then two days chopping it out with hoes, since nobody could expect the neighbors to take care of the weeds.

It was good to be home. Gas was hard to come by, so they parked the Chrysler next to the John Deere and only drove it on special occasions. They named their baby Grace Laurel after Williams's mother, who had died slowly, and Crystal's, who had died suddenly. With their tobacco money they bought a mule, traveling a hundred miles south to Muscle Shoals, Nova Africa, where the best ones were raised, and bringing it home in a borrowed trailer. Once a year, they sold their tobacco in Owensboro, where nobody had ever heard of Hey Hoss, and ate barbecued mutton and went dancing. They lived happily ever after.

As for Williams, he never got in any trouble about the Mustang or the credit card, for they had never existed. He mourned his fingertips, which had never existed, for about a month or two. Twice a year he turned over the engine on the tractor by hand, to keep it from rusting, and checked the lid on the jar, which he kept in the shed. Once a year he took the "yellowboy" into the woods for a deer.

As for Crystal, she learned to plow with a mule, but she never liked it as much as that old John Deere "A," which always reminded her of her father, Talking Man, and their auto trip to the North Pole.